Rascal
DOES NOT DREAM
of
His
Student

HAJIME
KAMOSHIDA

Illustration by
KEJI MIZOGUCHI

"Himeji's joining my class today."

"Hey, Yamada. And Yoshiwa!"

Sara Himeji

First-year at Minegahara High, a straight-A student. Chose Sakuta as her teacher at the cram school.

Sakuta Azusagawa

Kento Yamada

First-year at Minegahara, Sakuta's student at the cram school. Sara is in his class, and he's got a thing for her.

Juri Yoshiwa

Likewise, a Minegahara first-year in Sakuta's cram school class. On a beach volleyball team.

Mai Sakurajima

They were at a hot springs in Hakone.
A peaceful moment.

And they wanted to savor it.
Mai and Sakuta.

They'd been happy.
They were happy.

Chapter 1   December Gift ···································· 001

Chapter 2   Secrets and Promises ···················· 051

Chapter 3   I Need You ··· 103

Chapter 4   December 24 ····································· 159

Last Chapter Holy Night ··· 195

Rascal

DOES NOT DREAM
of
His
Student

Hajime Kamoshida

Illustration by
Keji Mizoguchi

YEN
ON

New York

Rascal Does Not Dream of His Student
Hajime Kamoshida

Translation by Andrew Cunningham
Cover art by Keji Mizoguchi

SEISHUN BUTA YARO WA MY STUDENT NO YUME WO MINAI Vol. 12
©Hajime Kamoshida 2022
Edited by Dengeki Bunko
First published in Japan in 2022 by KADOKAWA CORPORATION, Tokyo. English translation rights arranged with KADOKAWA CORPORATION, Tokyo through TUTTLE-MORI AGENCY, INC., Tokyo.

Yen On
150 West 30th Street, 19th Floor
New York, NY 10001

Visit us at yenpress.com
facebook.com/yenpress
twitter.com/yenpress
yenpress.tumblr.com
instagram.com/yenpress

First Yen On Edition: November 2023
Edited by Yen On Editorial: Ivan Liang
Designed by Yen Press Design: Andy Swist

Yen On is an imprint of Yen Press, LLC.
The Yen On name and logo are trademarks of Yen Press, LLC.

Library of Congress Cataloging-in-Publication Data
Names: Kamoshida, Hajime, 1978– author. | Mizoguchi, Keji, illustrator.
Title: Rascal does not dream of bunny girl senpai / Hajime Kamoshida ; illustration by Keji Mizoguchi.
Other titles: Seishun buta yarō. English
Description: New York, NY : Yen On, 2020. |
Contents: v. 1. Rascal does not dream of bunny girl senpai —
v. 2. Rascal does not dream of petite devil kohai —
v. 3. Rascal does not dream of logical witch —
v. 4. Rascal does not dream of siscon idol —
v. 5. Rascal does not dream of a sister home alone —
v. 6. Rascal does not dream of a dreaming girl —
v. 7. Rascal does not dream of his first love —
v. 8. Rascal does not dream of a sister venturing out —
v. 9. Rascal does not dream of a knapsack kid —
v. 10. Rascal does not dream of a lost singer —
v. 11. Rascal does not dream of a nightingale —
v. 12. Rascal does not dream of his student
Identifiers: LCCN 2020004455 | ISBN 9781975399351 (v. 1 ; trade paperback) |
ISBN 9781975312541 (v. 2 ; trade paperback) | ISBN 9781975312565 (v. 3 ; trade paperback) |
ISBN 9781975312589 (v. 4 ; trade paperback) | ISBN 9781975312602 (v. 5 ; trade paperback) |
ISBN 9781975312626 (v. 6 ; trade paperback) | ISBN 9781975312640 (v. 7 ; trade paperback) |
ISBN 9781975312664 (v. 8 ; trade paperback) | ISBN 9781975312688 (v. 9 ; trade paperback) |
ISBN 9781975318512 (v. 10 ; trade paperback) | ISBN 9781975343507 (v. 11 ; trade paperback) |
ISBN 9781975375270 (v. 12 ; trade paperback)
Subjects: CYAC: Fantasy.
Classification: LCC PZ7.1.K218 Ras 2020 | DDC [Fic]—dc23
LC record available at https://lccn.loc.gov/2020004455

ISBNs: 978-1-9753-7527-0 (paperback)
978-1-9753-7528-7 (ebook)

10 9 8 7 6 5 4 3 2 1

LSC-C

Printed in the United States of America

Where are you now? Who are you with? What's on your mind?
I'm alone at home. With my cat. Thinking of you.

But I'm not lonely. I'm not sad. The tears aren't flowing.
Not choking up, not hurting, not suffocating.
So come on…

Let me know (I don't wanna know) who you love.
I have to know (I don't wanna know) about the one I love.

Touko Kirishima, "I Need You"

Chapter
1
December Gift

1

One day, Sakuta Azusagawa received a new student at the cram school where he worked.

He'd attended classes till fourth period, then ridden the trains back to Fujisawa Station. When he reached the school, it was after six, and the sun was down. The real winter chill was setting in, the days were growing shorter, and the nights were arriving sooner.

He stashed his things in a staff locker and donned a white jacket—the mark of a teacher. He left the locker room carrying just the materials he planned to use in class, only for the principal to call him over.

"Azusagawa, good timing."

"Good morning."

Like the restaurant he also worked at, they used this greeting even at night.

"Yes, morning. I've got a student I'd like you to take charge of. Starting today, if that's okay?"

"Today? That's sudden."

"Her preference. You know Sara Himeji?"

He did. She'd sat in on his class once before.

"What do you say, Azusagawa?"

He had no good reason to refuse. He got paid on a per-student basis, so he'd been hoping to get more.

Sara was still a first-year. There was no need to scramble in preparation for college exams. Arguably, she was Sakuta's ideal type of student.

"All right."

"Okay, good, good."

As they wrapped up, a girl's voice called from the self-study cubicles. "Hey, Teach!"

Sakuta knew that Minegahara uniform all too well. She wore hers like a model student—the very girl they'd just been talking about, Sara Himeji.

She'd been studying while she waited for him.

The way she came running up to Sakuta reminded him of a friendly cat.

"Can't wait to learn, Azusagawa-sensei!" she said, bowing politely, hands straight at her sides.

Perhaps because the principal was watching, she even addressed him properly.

"Glad to have you, Himeji."

It was nice getting a new student without having to start from square one. And since her school was his alma mater, he had a pretty good grasp on what was being covered in her classes and even what was likely to show up on midterms and finals. He'd been a student there himself just a year before.

"Just do what you always do, Azusagawa."

"Will do."

With that, the principal went back to his own desk, muttering, "Now I've just got to submit the accounting paperwork and review the applications—augh, so much to do!"

Sara tore her eyes off his back and turned to Sakuta.

"Thanks for taking me on!" she said, bowing again the moment their eyes met.

"Don't mention it. Thanks to you, my wage is going up."

"Make sure my *grades* go up," she said, making a pouty face.

This girl was sharp enough to riff off his dumb jokes. But seeing her here was a powerful reminder of the dream he'd had a few days earlier.

A very vivid dream, one that didn't feel like a dream at all.

A dream in which Sara became his student on December 1.

And make no mistake—today *was* December 1.

The principal's call, the way he'd brought up a new student, and the timing with which Sara's head had popped up from the study booth, even the words they'd just exchanged—all matched the dream exactly.

It felt like watching a recording of these exact moments. It was a bit like the time he and Tomoe Koga had been stuck in a loop back during his second year of high school. Only far shorter.

For that reason, the true cause of these dreams eluded him, leaving him more baffled than shocked. It was a weird sensation, like he'd been left behind—a feeling he couldn't quite shake.

The world felt wobbly beneath his feet, and he couldn't settle himself.

If the dream version had felt that real—how could he know he wasn't dreaming *now*? That seemed just as likely. There was next to no discernable differences between the dream and reality.

"Teach?" Sara prompted, crooking her head.

"Mm?"

"If you've got nothing to say, you shouldn't just stare."

She put her hands over her face, hiding from him.

"Oh, sorry."

He hadn't been looking *at* her, but his gaze had been aimed in her direction.

He turned toward the school entrance—just as Kento Yamada came in with a very unenthusiastic greeting, saying "'Sup."

Juri Yoshiwa was right behind him. "Hello."

Sakuta was teaching math to these kids. Like Sara, they were both Minegahara students. Kento was even in the same class as her.

"Oh, perfect timing, you arrived together. Turns out…"

Before he could tell them about Sara…

"We ran into each other on the elevator."

Juri's correction was a bit forced. Saying "Right" here seemed weird, so Sakuta just sort of awkwardly nodded.

"Himeji's joining my class today. Figured you should know."

"Hey, Yamada. And Yoshiwa!"

"Oh? Legit?" Kento was very obviously rattled by this news, but not in an unwelcoming way. He had a crush on Sara, so this was entirely a good thing for him—it had just caught him off guard. And left him unable to disguise his reaction.

"Yamada, what's that supposed to mean?" Sara asked, giving him a searching look.

"Er, what do *you* mean?" he asked evasively.

"Legit good? Or legit bad?" she pressed.

"Neither!" He turned his back on her, fidgeting.

Sara put her hands to her mouth, stifling a giggle.

Juri brushed past the two of them like this was none of her concern. She headed right to the booth where they held classes.

"Sakuta-sensei, start the class!" Kento said, red-faced. "It's time!"

"I have *never* seen you this motivated, Yamada."

Kento ignored Sakuta's remark as he chased after Juri.

So transparent. And his reaction had *also* been part of Sakuta's dream. The same went for Juri's impassive response.

Which raised more questions.

If this had just been a one-off bit of weirdness Sakuta alone went through, then he'd have laughed it off eventually.

But he knew full well that wasn't the case.

Similar stories were showing up all over the internet, tagged #dreaming.

The town was abuzz with tales of dreams come true.

Ikumi Akagi had been actively using the hashtag to save people, which made it impossible to dismiss these incidents as mere superstition. Sakuta had seen a #dreaming post come true—seen it with his own eyes.

Once that happened, he *had* to believe.

On a daily basis, there were hundreds of posts with that hashtag.

All of them described dreams from the night before.

Everyone was excitedly wondering if they'd come true.

More appeared every day.

Plenty of people were dismissive or mocked the idea, and there were more than a few arguments raging about how seriously these posts should be treated.

Was it a portent? Or was something already going wrong?

Now that it directly involved him, Sakuta couldn't exactly feign indifference.

And worst of all—he had a hunch who might have caused all this.

Touko Kirishima.

Many knew her as a popular Internet singer who uploaded her work to video-sharing sites.

To Sakuta, she was a mysterious miniskirt Santa only he could see.

He'd have to get some answers out of her the next time they met.

And he had good reason why he *had* to track her down.

——*Find Touko Kirishima.*

——*Mai's in danger.*

A message from a better Sakuta from another potential world.

Once he'd seen that—

—he couldn't just leave it alone.

He had to find out what it meant. No matter what.

Still, fretting about it now wouldn't get him any close to Touko.

Here at work, all he could do was teach these kids math.

Sara was still hanging out by the staff area, so he said, "It is about time. Let's get started."

"Okay! Can't wait to learn, Teach!"

At Minegahara High, final exams started the next day. And the math exam was on the first day, which suited Sakuta just fine. He was planning on making sure they knew how to handle their trigonometry.

2

The eighty-minute lesson over with, Sakuta bade his students good luck on the exam and sent them packing.

"Sakuta-sensei, don't remind me!" Kento said, scowling at him.

Juri simply bobbed her head—this could be either yes or no—and vanished through the doors.

It seemed it would be a while before he earned trust or respect.

"Don't worry—*I'll* do well," Sara said. That was nice of her.

He'd asked her to hang back to discuss class scheduling and the lesson plans.

"We'll probably spend the next class mostly reviewing anything the three of you got wrong on the test, but…what are you hoping for after that, Himeji?"

She was a bright kid and immediately understood what he had left unsaid.

What he was teaching now wasn't enough for her.

Sakuta's lesson plan was designed to help shore up Kento's and Juri's fundamentals. But Sara already knew all those.

It wouldn't do her much good to sit through the same lectures.

She thought about it for a minute, then looked right at him.

"Can I decide after the exams are done?"

"Of course."

"I don't wanna sound too cocky and then get a thirty on the finals," she said, fighting back a smile.

"Better not joke about that in front of Yamada."

Kento had scored exactly thirty on the midterms. And Sara had seen that answer sheet—chances were good that she was referencing that grade directly.

"Don't tell him I was picking on him. This is…a secret between the two of us, Teach."

Her smile bubbled over. She seemed quite pleased he'd gotten her joke.

"Then you'll stick to the same day as them next time?"

"For the exam review? Sure."

"You might not have your answer sheets back, but bring a copy of the test itself."

"Got it. We can talk about the future again, then."

"Mm. Take care on your way home."

Sara shouldered her backpack. But she didn't make a move to the door. She was looking up at him like she wanted him to say something else.

"You're not gonna wish me luck on the exam?"

"I *know* you'll get a good grade."

"Way to turn up the pressure!"

Her words made it sound like she was upset, but her sunny smile suggested otherwise. She sailed out the doors.

Once she was gone, Sakuta filed the report on the day's class. Since there was an extra student listed, he had more to write.

Once the necessary paperwork was out of the way, he looked around for Rio Futaba, who also worked here part-time. If her class was over, he figured they could leave together, giving him a chance to pick her brain about dreams coming true.

He found Rio readily enough; she was in the common area near the staff room, answering the questions of a rather tall boy—Toranosuke Kasai, who studied physics with her.

She had one finger on an open textbook and was scribbling in a notebook with her other hand. Each time Rio asked "With me so far?" he said "Yes" so softly it was hard to believe it came from a body that big. She finished one problem and moved on to the next.

This seemed like it could take a while.

It wasn't like the dream thing *had* to be discussed today. He could wait.

The threat to Mai was much more urgent, and he'd consulted Rio about it the same day he got the message.

He'd straight up borrowed Mai's phone to call her and had her meet him at Fujisawa Station as soon as her classes were over. They'd discussed the situation at the family restaurant that was Sakuta's other workplace.

"All I can say now is that there's two main categories of threat," Rio said, returning from the drink counter with a coffee.

"And those are?"

"Touko Kirishima herself is a danger to Sakurajima."

"Or?"

"Someone who got Adolescence Syndrome from Touko Kirishima will put Sakurajima in harm's way."

"Yeah, one or the other."

The warning was so short all they could really deduce from it was these nebulous findings.

There was no indication of what would happen, what the threat was, or even what kind of peril they were facing.

All they knew was that it was somehow connected to Touko Kirishima.

"No matter how I think about it, the direct-threat angle doesn't seem very likely."

That would just be a crime. He couldn't come up with a possible motive. None of their meetings had suggested there was any deep-seated resentment. And since she was invisible, she'd had no shortage

of opportunity. The fact that nothing had happened to Mai so far proved him right.

"I agree the latter option is more likely."

But that didn't completely rule out the former. Rio took a sip of coffee, leaving that conclusion unsaid.

At most, Touko had once sounded irritated by Mai's arrival. But that was arguably just a reaction to having their conversation interrupted. Even if there was more to it, it hadn't felt strong enough to justify committing a crime.

"What do you think I should do, Futaba?" he asked, once she'd put her cup down.

Sakuta felt like he lacked enough information to take any decisive action.

"If you want to cut the problem off at its source, then cure Touko Kirishima's Adolescence Syndrome."

Only Sakuta could see her.

Just like how only he'd been able to see Mai.

"That's *your* department."

The smile on Rio's lips suggested she was recalling how he'd solved Mai's problem.

The moment he'd asked Mai out.

He'd run out on the field during a test and yelled "I love you!" for the whole school to hear.

"If only that solved everything."

Sadly, Mai and Touko were very different. Not just his relationship to them, but the why and the how.

They'd known enough about why Mai was disappearing that Rio had been able to put together a working hypothesis, but they still knew next to nothing about Touko.

Why couldn't anyone else see her?

The similarities to Mai's symptoms only emphasized the differences.

Touko had merely vanished from the visible spectrum. Where Mai had vanished from people's memories, everyone still knew who Touko was.

They were listening to the songs she uploaded and talking about how much they loved her and her music.

"Futaba, do you think she's actually causing this latest round of Adolescence Syndrome?"

Touko had described that as giving out "presents."

Like how Uzuki Hirokawa had suddenly learned to read the room.

Or how Ikumi Akagi had swapped places with another potential self.

As for the students dreaming of the future...she'd called those presents, too. Apparently those were the gifts everyone wanted.

"She said so herself."

And that was why Rio was suggesting that curing her Adolescence Syndrome would solve everything else.

"On the other hand, all we have is her word for it."

And no actual proof. He and Rio could sit here speculating for hours and get nowhere. The path forward was already closed.

"I guess you're right, then."

Standing at the dead end did bring him to one conclusion. It prepared him to accept the task.

"I'll just have to cure Touko Kirishima."

Rio agreed with a meaningful look.

"Might be some small comfort, but keep an eye on the dreaming hashtag. Maybe one post will give you a clue."

"An eye for an eye, a tooth for a tooth, and Adolescence Syndrome for Adolescence Syndrome."

When he got home, he put Rio's advice into action. He borrowed his sister Kaede's laptop and pored over all the #dreaming posts for anything about Mai Sakurajima. He found exactly zero stories that seemed connected to any overt danger.

Ever since, he began routinely searching the hashtag.

*   *   *

As long as Sakuta maintained a good pace, the walk home took maybe ten minutes. After class ended, Sakuta made it back to his apartment just after nine.

"I'm home!"

He took off his shoes and stepped up inside. Their cat, Nasuno, came padding out from the living room. A moment later, the washroom door opened.

"Oh, Sakuta. Welcome back."

It was his sister, Kaede, in her pajamas.

She headed into the kitchen, still drying her hair. He heard the freezer door open, so she must have been in a mood for a cold treat.

He took over the washroom to wash his hands and gargle. Then he headed into the living room, allowing himself to feel a little hopeful.

His eyes snapped to the answering machine.

He was waiting for a callback. Desperate for it.

But the red light held steady. It would be flashing if someone had left a message. He checked the call logs, but nobody had phoned them.

"Guess I'll try again."

He punched in the newest number in his mental telephone directory.

The one the miniskirt Santa had given him.

A moment later, he heard it ringing.

That proved the number was in use.

If she was telling the truth, this should be Touko Kirishima's cell phone.

After the seventh ring, it sent him to voice mail. It was the same default message he'd heard several times over the last few days.

He hadn't just called once or twice. He'd left a voice mail the day before, as well.

There was no sign of her calling him back, but Sakuta didn't let that discourage him. Once more, he spoke into the receiver.

"Is this Touko Kirishima's number? This is Sakuta Azusagawa, calling to learn more about Santa Claus. Hope you'll call me back."

With that, he hung up.

From behind him, Kaede scoffed. "What was that, a prank call?"

He turned around and found her giving him a look of great suspicion, an orange Popsicle in her mouth.

"Not a prank. Just a normal call."

"You've totally lost it!"

"Kaede, you're starting to sound like a high school girl."

"Your fault for always being weird."

"Yeah?"

"The fact you don't even realize how bad you are means you're already insane."

Their sibling banter was suddenly interrupted.

The phone was ringing.

Not Kaede's cell phone, but the landline.

An eleven-digit number was on the display. It was a number he didn't yet recognize instantly but *did* know.

He grabbed the receiver.

"Azusagawa speaking."

He opened with the most ordinary greeting.

"……"

No response came.

But he could hear someone on the other end.

"Kirishima, right?"

The number on the screen proved as much.

"You're smarter than you look," Touko said, somehow managing to make it not sound like a compliment.

He had a hunch what she meant.

She'd flashed that number at him for three seconds total and was taking a dig at him for managing to memorize it.

"I get that a lot."

"And downright devious."

This was probably a warning not to keep playing dumb. Or maybe it referred to how he'd pretended he *hadn't* learned her number. Possibly both.

"And yet awfully stupid."

His reputation seemed to be in free fall. But it hadn't exactly started out high. It had only seemed that way because she'd called him smart. What she'd meant by it was less flattering.

"If you call someone and they don't answer, most people would work out they're being ghosted."

"I figured it's fair play till you block the number."

He had good reason not to just let it drop.

——*Find Touko Kirishima.*

——*Mai's in danger.*

The other Sakuta had told him this.

"I got questions, Kirishima."

"How to become Santa Claus? That's a secret."

"Can we meet again?"

He definitely didn't expect to get much out of a single phone call.

There was too much he didn't know.

He'd been told to find Touko and had her on the line—he'd also met her in person. Arguably, he'd *already* found her.

But that didn't bring him any closer to finding out why "Mai's in danger."

Like Rio said, right now they only had two working theories.

Touko harming Mai herself.

Or the threat coming from someone who'd received a gift of Adolescence Syndrome from the miniskirt Santa.

One or the other.

But even that was just conjecture.

For that reason, he wanted to meet her in person, gauge her responses with his own eyes.

"It's December now," she said.

His eyes turned to the calendar. "So it seems."

Only one month left in the year.

"This is a busy time for Santa Claus."

"Can you squeeze me in?"

"How about tomorrow?"

"Uh, actually, tomorrow isn't…"

Today was December 1. Which meant the next day was December 2—a special day that came once a year.

"Call again after classes are over. If I feel like it, I might meet up with you."

Touko wasn't listening to him sputter.

"It can't be another day?"

He was clutching at straws.

"You have other plans?" she asked, sounding annoyed.

"It's my girlfriend's birthday."

Mai had secured a rare day off and said, "I've got somewhere I want to take you, Sakuta. Don't make plans after class." He'd been looking forward to that birthday date ever since.

"Oh," Touko said, apparently convinced.

Perhaps that meant she'd agree to change plans.

But that hope was soon dashed.

"Then I'm *definitely* not meeting you any other day."

There was a mocking lilt in her voice.

And she hung up immediately.

He couldn't even try to stop her.

He tried calling back.

"……"

Shockingly, she didn't pick up.

All he got was the voice mail.

"This is Azusagawa calling to discuss tomorrow, will call again."

With that, he hung up.

"Sakuta, these prank calls are going too far," Kaede said, dropping her Popsicle stick in the trash.

"I'm calling to make sure things *don't* go too far."

Now how was he supposed to break this to Mai?

She'd likely understand if he told the truth. She was familiar with the circumstances. But he didn't think she'd *like* it.

"Guess I'd better go to bed early."

The next day was gonna take a lot out of him.

He'd need stamina to weather his tongue-lashing.

3

"Fine. We'll just cancel today's plans."

Mai's answer came the next day, while Sakuta sat in the passenger seat of her car.

They were stopped at a red light during a momentary lull in the hum of traffic, only the two of them on board. They were heading in for second-period classes. Nodoka had a first-period class, so for once she wasn't hanging around underfoot.

"We'll have that date some other time."

Mai's hand left the wheel and brushed a lock of hair behind her shoulder.

"Aww."

"You're the one who changed plans, so I'm not sure why you're upset."

"I was really looking forward to it."

"That's my line."

The light turned green, so instead of stomping his foot, she hit the gas a bit hard. The car shot forward.

"I was hoping you'd be disappointed."

"I am. Very much so."

She shot him a baleful side-eye. The moment she'd said hello, he'd noticed her makeup game was even more on point than usual.

"All my preparations went for naught."

Even her clothes had clearly been chosen with the birthday date in mind.

She was wearing gray wide-legged slacks with a center crease that beautifully accentuated her silhouette. The waist portion was tucked in like a drawstring pouch, further enhancing Mai's figure. And her white blouse was simple but stylish.

All in all, her look today was less "cute" and more "elegant and classy."

A black coat to wear out and about lay on the back seat.

"I'm always happy to spend time with my gorgeous Mai."

"*Happy* isn't the word I'd use."

A powerful counter.

Perhaps it'd be best to stop poking that wound.

"It is what it is," she admitted. There was a good reason for all this. She was actively being targeted.

That was the sole reason she had agreed to cancel the birthday date so readily. Why she'd said "Fine" without a hint of fury.

Part of him was glad, but any sense of relief he felt was far outweighed by his own frustrations.

After the warning they'd received, Mai *must* have been anxious.

If the other world's Sakuta had sent a warning, this wasn't about tripping over a pebble or stubbing her toe on a doorjamb. Nothing so ordinary fit the bill.

It was safe to assume a much bigger threat was bearing down on her.

The two of them had already lived through the worst-case scenario— that day in the snow. Hearing that Mai was in danger just brought back those unpleasant memories.

It might not be *this* body that had lived through that, but everything that went down on Christmas Eve had been carved into the back of his mind. The horror he felt as the snow turned red was still fresh in his mind. Not that he planned to forget it; this was a pain that must never be forgotten and would always remain in Sakuta's heart.

And the same was likely true for Mai.

So why did she show no signs of it?

"Be grateful you have an understanding girlfriend."

"If it means I spend less time with you, I don't *want* to be grateful."

"Should I come along?"

"That won't fly."

He said that a bit too forcefully.

Sakuta didn't think Touko Kirishima personally meant Mai any harm. He didn't—but there was still a thorn in his heart making him wary, and that had come out in his voice. He'd let it out.

And by the time he realized his mistake, it was too late.

Mai'd been painstakingly trying to act like they always did, and one word from him had shattered that mood. In an instant, it became so tense that it was almost palpable.

Sakuta couldn't see a way to quickly salvage the situation. He regretted everything, and his eyes fled to the side-view mirror.

Then Mai chuckled.

"Don't sweat it," she said.

"I am."

"I know you're worried."

Mai's eyes lighted briefly on the Christmassy colors of a convenience store's display.

"It's almost Christmas," she said.

He really couldn't get anything past her. Any other time of year, Sakuta probably could have kept it together.

But ever since his memories came back, the arrival of the Christmas season did a number on him. The whole town turned red and green, lights everywhere—and that left him with an indescribable sense of loss and panic.

"I'll spend as much time with you as I can this month."

"Right now I want to be together from good morning to good night."

He didn't even want to go outside at all. Staying put at home would be just fine by him.

——*Mai's in danger.*

Until the meaning of that sentence came to light.

He didn't want to lose Mai again. Couldn't bear that happening twice.

But locking Mai up at home was hardly realistic. She had college and work. If a famous actress suddenly dropped out of sight, that would mean only bad news. It'd be a totally different kind of danger.

"Oh? Only right now?"

"Even when right now ends."

"If you can joke, you're fine."

"You aren't anxious at all, Mai?"

"I've got you, so I'm okay."

That was a real heart-skipper, and she made it sound so obvious.

"Uh, Mai."

"Mm?"

"Can we pull over at the next store?"

"Why?"

"So I can hug you."

The seat belts made that hard while driving.

"Absolutely not."

"Aww."

Mai was laughing happily.

Just being with her did a lot to calm his nerves. The anxiety didn't exactly go away—but he also couldn't let it show. He didn't want to dump this all on Mai.

Today, he'd just have to meet Touko and get some answers.

"So where was it you wanted to take me, Mai?"

"You'll find out once we're there."

"Potential wedding venues?"

"No."

"Meet and greet with your mom?"

"You did that already." Mai scoffed. Her eyes were on the road sign above.

The car passed under the blue-and-white guide sign. Like an idea had just struck her, Mai changed the subject.

"Sakuta, what's your second-period class?"

"Core curriculum."

"You're good on attendance?"

"I'm not *you*."

"I'm good on that, too."

The Sekiya Interchange was fast approaching. It wasn't technically an interchange at all, just an intersection with multiple roads that *looked* like an interchange.

As they drew close, Mai put her blinker on and turned left. To get to their college, she would have to go straight—onto Loop 4. This was hardly the first time she'd driven them in, so Sakuta was starting to learn the route.

"Mai?"

His question was obvious.

"……"

Mai didn't answer. She just kept driving down a whole new road. Eventually, it connected to National Route 1. They followed that to the Totsuka Interchange and then merged onto the expressway.

The guide signs were starting to mention places toward Yokohama proper. Sakuta and Mai went to college in Kanazawa-hakkei. That was technically part of Yokohama, but in a very different direction from the places around Yokohama Station these signs referred to. They were a solid twenty minutes away by train.

"Are we playing hooky?"

When Mai was able to attend classes, she always went, however brief a time that might be. This was possibly the first time he'd ever seen her intentionally bail.

"It's my birthday, so I'll do what I want."

Mai seemed to be enjoying herself quite a bit as she adjusted her grip on the wheel. It would be a full half hour before Sakuta learned the reason why.

Mai pulled into the basement parking lot below Landmark Tower, the signature building of Yokohama's Minato Mirai district.

By this point, Sakuta was already sensing trouble. He was the one in danger now.

"Mai, why are we here?"

"Follow me, and you'll find out."

They left the car and got on an elevator.

Mai pressed the button for the third floor.

The bell signaled their arrival, and the doors opened. A vast shopping mall stood before them.

The wide-open space gave it a relaxing vibe. Even the people walking around seemed extra chill.

"Here," Mai said, stopping outside an especially upscale shop.

The name was written in English, yet Sakuta still recognized it.

It was a world-famous jewelry store known for their signature shade of blue.

It had even been used in the title of an old movie.

Sakuta felt his jaw drop.

"A lovely gift from my boyfriend would be the perfect way to celebrate turning twenty. Agreed?"

"…Agreed."

She had a point, and he had no choice.

"Just…"

But he was already walking it back, his defense mechanisms kicking in.

"Just what?" Mai asked, with her sweetest smile. Her head tilted ever so slightly as she peered into his eyes.

Not fair. Not at all fair, but it completely cut off any avenue of retreat.

"Can it double as a Christmas present?"

That was as far as he could go.

"My mother used to say that when I was young, and I always hated it."

But despite her words, Mai was smiling. Sakuta's lips were turned in the exact opposite direction, but she went on ahead and entered the shop.

He just had to commit.

"Good thing I brought cash for this date…"

Grateful for his foresight in withdrawing his wages the day before, Sakuta followed her in.

His first step into the shop was one to remember.

The instant he crossed the threshold, it felt like the very air had changed. Even the smell was different. He was half convinced the ground beneath his feet was not the same.

The graceful interior had a modest number of display cases. It was quite spacious, so they could have put far more on display but chose not to.

It was a luxurious use of space. There was no avoiding the staff's attention and hiding in the shelves here. Or disappearing into the crowd of customers—there was only one other couple in the store. There were more staff than clients.

Thus, the moment they stepped in, a gracefully composed lady greeted them. She was maybe in her late twenties and came toward them with a smile. That polished business demeanor did not last for very long.

"What brings you here…?!"

She broke off, surprised. She managed to avoid a squeak, but her lips made it clear that it was a very close call. Her entire body froze for a brief second.

The cause was obvious. *The* Mai Sakurajima stood before her.

She soon recovered her smile. "Pardon me," she said. "Would you care to use a table in the back?"

She was leaning in, speaking softly so the other couple wouldn't hear.

"Sorry for the unannounced visit. That would be appreciated."

Mai had donned her public-figure face.

Sakuta was feeling more and more out of place here. Nothing about this store helped put him at ease.

"We don't want to bother *them*," Mai said, taking Sakuta's elbow.

"This way," the staff lady said, ushering them into a space that was less a "table" than a private room. There *was* a table in it, so she hadn't technically been wrong.

In lieu of chairs, they had an upright couch.

He and Mai sat down together.

The lady introduced herself and explained her role at the store. Sakuta certainly got the impression that if they'd come this far, leaving empty-handed was no longer an option.

"What are you looking for?" the lady asked, looking at Mai.

Mai glanced at Sakuta, so that business smile turned his way.

"Today's Mai's birthday," he said. "Her twentieth."

"Well, happy birthday."

Mai acknowledged this with a nod.

"And I wanted to get her a present."

The lady was nodding enthusiastically, which made him squirm.

"Do you have anything one can buy on a college student's part-time wages?"

There was no point playing games about it, so he put forth the vital info right away. He'd caught a glimpse of those display cases out front, and the price tags had been downright shocking.

"We have many lovely pieces to choose from. Why don't I pick out a few for you to look at?"

"Please."

"I'll be right back."

She bowed her head and took her leave.

Only when the door closed did Sakuta let himself lean back against the seat.

"Haaah…" The sigh escaped him.

Before he had a chance to take another breath, there was a knock, and another lady came in. Two seconds after he'd leaned back, Sakuta was bolt upright again.

"Here you are," she said, placing steaming-hot teacups before them. Inside was clear liquid the color of brand-new bricks. Even from here, it smelled good.

"Thank you," Mai said.

"Enjoy," the lady said, and she bowed herself out.

The first lady came in as the second one left.

She returned holding two trays.

"Thank you for waiting," she said.

Not enough time had passed for it to really be called a wait. If anything, Sakuta would've actually preferred she take a bit longer, giving him a moment to settle down.

She smoothly shifted the teacups to the sides of the table and placed the first tray between them.

There were three necklaces laid out in gray felt cases. One had a heart shape dangling from it. One ran through a ring. And one featured a four-leaf clover motif.

"Oh," Mai said, reaching for one.

She picked up the necklace with the four-leaf clover.

"You wore that in a movie last year," the lady said. "Quite a few customers came here after seeing that, hoping to own the same piece."

She put the other tray down.

This one had three rings on it.

One looked like linked leaves, one had two rings crossed, and the last matched the heart on the first necklace.

All of them gleamed a beautiful shade of silver.

"Try on anything you like."

Mai reached right for the heart-shaped ring.

It fit perfectly on her right ring finger.

One look at it, and her eyes softened. A smile spilled out onto her face.

"Well?" she asked, showing Sakuta her finger, clearly pleased.

The heart-shaped ring inarguably looked great on Mai's long, slender finger. It fit so perfectly it seemed like it had always been there.

"It looks amazing," he said. There was no other possible response.

"It absolutely does," the lady said, catching the ball. She started telling Mai more about the ring, but Sakuta heard none of it.

His eyes were locked on the unobtrusive price tag.

Gallingly, it was significantly more reasonable than what he'd imagined. As ordered, she'd brought something he could afford on his earnings.

"What do you think?"

Mai passed the look from the lady to Sakuta.

The present was from him, so clearly the choice was his—and he was pressed to make one.

"I definitely like the heart motif," he said. "Both types."

There was a necklace and a ring, and they matched.

The lady shifted things around so both pieces were on the same tray. Everything else was on the other.

The ring on the right.

The necklace on the left.

A binary choice, laid out visually.

All he had to do was choose.

He looked at the ring again.

It gleamed.

He checked out the necklace.

It was shiny.

The ring's price tag was noticeably higher.

He quietly took a deep breath.

Then another.

Then he said, "I'll go with this one," and pointed at his choice.

"Please come again!"

The lady escorted Sakuta and Mai through the shop and bowed them out the door.

They moved away, walking toward the elevator together.

Mai's hand was in his, and on it was the heart-shaped silver ring.

They'd had her size in stock, so she'd worn it out.

"You heard the lady," Mai said, teasing him.

"I guess the next one'll be our engagement ring."

"I suppose I can look forward to that."

He would probably have to add a zero to the price tag.

"Oh, Mai…"

"Mm?"

"Happy birthday."

"Sakuta…"

"Mm?"

"You always say that too late."

"Next year I wanna say it to your face the moment the date changes."

"That'll depend on my work schedule."

But Mai gave their clasped hands a little swing.

4

After their detour, Sakuta and Mai reached the college with only twenty minutes left on the lunch break.

The cafeteria was starting to empty, and students who'd finished eating were killing time before their next class. The campus was as it ever was.

Sakuta ordered the soba soup on the grounds that it would come out fast and could be eaten quickly for less than 300 yen.

He'd just dropped a wad of cash, so hot soup warmed the wallet and his heart.

Not that he was regretting today's shopping trip.

On the way into the college, Mai had looked down at the ring on her finger at every red light, practically overflowing with joy.

They'd been dating for two and a half years, and he'd never seen her like this. No matter how hard she tried, there was no way to keep her emotion from showing on her face.

Maybe he should have given her a ring earlier—he almost regretted *that*, instead.

Sakuta sat down at an empty table, and Mai took the seat next to him once her soup was ready. She'd gone one step fancier than him and ordered hers with tempura.

Mai grabbed that tempura with her chopsticks and dropped it in Sakuta's bowl.

"My way of saying thanks."

"In that case, you'll have to feed it to me."

Mai ignored his griping and started slurping up her soba.

They didn't have much time before third period, so he gave up and tore into the tempura. There was a satisfying crunch.

Neither said much as they focused on finishing their meals in time.

Sakuta drained the last drop of soup, letting the smell of the *katsuo* broth regale his nostrils. As he was savoring an underlying hint of soy sauce—

"Azusagawa."

—someone called his name. He looked up from the bowl and found Ikumi Akagi standing across the table from him.

Her eyes met Mai's, and she bobbed her head. Then she turned her eyes back to Sakuta, looking rueful.

"Sorry, I'm still getting nothing."

She showed them her palm.

Four days ago, that had been where the message from the other potential world appeared.

After seeing that, Sakuta had asked Ikumi for a favor.

His request was to communicate with the other world and find out what the message meant.

How was Mai in danger?

Why did he have to find Touko Kirishima?

With those answers, the problem was as good as solved.

He didn't know about the other Sakuta, but in this world—he'd already found Touko Kirishima.

He'd even arranged to meet up with her today.

But yesterday, the day before, and the day before that—there'd been no response to Ikumi's queries. Being the serious, diligent type, she'd come by to report that each day, looking deeply sorry about it each time.

"I think messages I write are no longer reaching the other me. Since I received that last message, our sensations haven't synced up once."

"Well, that's probably better for you, Akagi."

All that meant was that Ikumi's Adolescence Syndrome was fully cured.

"But…," she said, frowning.

He knew what she was about to say, so he jumped on top of it.

"Don't start feeling responsible and swapping places again. I've had enough things be my fault."

"......Fair. I'll be on the lookout."

She seemed less tense. She must have picked up on his humor. He wasn't sure if she really understood that he had been mostly serious.

Of course, *serious* was Ikumi Akagi's middle name.

She'd brought those messages to them, so she felt responsible. Probably even more than Sakuta imagined.

That was simply how her mind worked. It had been made painfully clear just the other day. He had to remain vigilant. Ikumi's promises and reassurances were little better than lip service.

"I'll be in touch if I do learn anything," she said, then bowed to Mai again and left their table.

Saki Kamisato was waiting for her by the cafeteria entrance. They exchanged a few words and headed off to class. By all appearances, they were still friends after the swap back.

That was probably good news for Ikumi. Saki had given Sakuta an irate glare, so probably not such great news for *him*.

The warning bell rang. Five minutes till classes began.

That prompted the lingering chatterers to their feet.

Sakuta and Mai returned their dishes and headed out.

"Will you be home this evening, Mai?"

"I'll be at your place."

"You really do dote on me."

"Nodoka's picking up a cake, so we figured we'd share it with Kaede."

She showed Sakuta the message history on her phone. He was *not* allowed to be pleased about the canceled date.

"She's asking if you need any."

"Tell her of course I do."

"Okay, Sakuta. You be careful."

They'd paused on the second-story landing. Mai's class was here, while Sakuta's was up another flight.

"You be even more careful, Mai."

"If anything happens to me, you'll cry."

"I absolutely will."

That answer seemed to please her. She waved the hand with the ring on it and went into her class.

"Mai is at her cutest today," Sakuta said, and he headed up the stairs, chewing on his own happiness.

And to ensure that happiness would continue—after classes, he was going to meet Santa Claus.

5

Fourth-period core curriculum ended ten minutes before the bell rang.

"It's a bit early, but that's all for today."

The professor piled up their things and left the room. Not one student complained about the early dismissal. They were already chatting with friends.

"Ready to hit the road?" Takumi Fukuyama asked. He was a friend of Sakuta's from class. He packed up and shouldered his backpack.

"Sorry, I got stuff to do."

"Another date? Jealous! You go have fun, then. Later!"

After delivering a dizzying array of emotions, Takumi stalked away.

"Boy needs to get a grip," Sakuta muttered.

Then someone else approached.

"Azusagawa, hola."

This greeting came from the international business major Miori Mitou. Since Sakuta was a statistical science major, their only classes in common were the core curriculum and their secondary foreign language course—Spanish.

"On your own today, Mitou?"

She usually left class with her female friends.

"Manami's crowd all skipped together."

"Just the girls?"

"And some guys."

"From the mixer you got lost on the way to?"

"Yep."

She seemed mildly miffed—had she been left out? Probably.

"Well, that's nice."

"Aggravating!"

She narrowed her eyes and lashed out at Sakuta, even though her other friends were to blame. For some reason, he always found that side of her likable.

"I mean, if you go, you'll snare all the boys' hearts and leave the other girls empty-handed."

"I am that bitch."

That sounded like both a joke *and* genuinely bitter.

At the very least, Miori was well aware of how other people saw her.

"Oh, and I saw Mai," she said, changing the subject and putting both hands on the desk, leaning in.

"That happens. She *does* go here."

"We had core English together third period. And her hand was all sparkly."

She was really playing that up to tease him.

"Was that a birthday present from you?"

"Mai didn't tell you?"

"She was radiating happiness too hard. I didn't dare ask. Rings sure are nice!"

Miori turned her gaze to the ceiling, rapturous.

This surprised Sakuta.

He found it hard to imagine her putting any special value on jewelry.

And that impression turned out pretty accurate.

Her next line revealed what was really going on here.

"*I* wanted to give Mai a present."

"You're more the type people give to."

"But I've got no one promising, so I wouldn't want any gifts to begin with."

Sakuta found this reasonable, more or less. She was checking to see if he'd followed, and he probably did. The gift giver and receiver each had their own feelings, and it was only enjoyable for everyone involved when those feelings aligned. There was no inherent meaning in the ring itself.

And Miori currently had no one she *wanted* a gift from.

"Oh, and my birthday—"

"Lines like that are why you're in demand."

He interrupted her to point out what was causing her problems. It was the right thing for him to do as a potential friend.

"I only talk like this with you, Azusagawa."

"And lines like that are why you're in demand." It's like she hadn't heard a single word he'd said.

"Then how *should* I talk to boys?" she asked grumpily. She almost made it seem like this was his fault.

"'Nice weather we're having'?"

"What's fun about *that*?"

Being boring was the point, but Miori didn't seem to get it.

At this point, a bell rang, indicating the end of fourth period.

"I've got a fifth—better run. *Chao!*"

Miori waved and left the room, tote bag in one hand.

Sakuta didn't watch her leave. He just got up and put his backpack on.

Once the bell rang, there was no time to waste.

Sakuta had promised to call Touko after class.

Miori aside, there weren't many students with fifth-period classes, so once fourth period ended, the campus vibe switched to "after class."

Students headed off to practice or clubs, or they rushed off to their jobs.

Sakuta left the building and found a throng headed down the tree-lined path toward the main gates.

He stepped out of that flow of people by the clock tower to use the public phones there.

Sakuta had never seen anyone else use them. They might as well have existed exclusively for him.

He lifted the receiver and dropped in a coin. He set a stack of ten-yen coins on top, just in case, and punched in eleven digits.

The call was picked up as soon as it rang.

At that speed, she'd likely been using the phone as it started ringing.

"Azusagawa speaking. I believe I have an appointment."

"I'm by the front gate."

She hung up without another word.

After collecting the unused coins, he left the phones behind.

He headed down the path to the main gate.

Not long after, he saw his destination through the crowd.

But a miniskirt Santa was nowhere to be found.

Even after going past the gates, he failed to locate Touko's red outfit.

"Should I just wait?"

But on the phone, she'd said she was already there.

Not sure what to make of her absence, Sakuta stepped off to the side.

And found someone already there.

Like him, they were waiting for someone?

She wore short culottes, black tights, and boots. On top, she had a shaggy sweater with a long coat over it.

Sakuta didn't want to get uncomfortably close, so he stopped a good five steps away and waited for Touko to show.

But for some reason, the girl called out to him.

"Is this a joke? Or just spite?"

He only worked it out when he placed her voice.

"Sorry to keep you waiting, Kirishima," he said, as if nothing had happened. "Turns out even Santa Claus wears street clothes."

Sakuta had just assumed he'd be meeting a miniskirt Santa, so he failed to spot her even though she was in plain sight. Even her makeup was a dramatic departure from her Santa style. The emphasized eyes had given way to a more natural look.

"If you're that dense, you must be a constant disappointment to that girlfriend of yours."

"Every now and then she tells me she loves me."

"This way."

Touko stalked away from the gates, clearly not in the mood for his boasting.

She turned away from Kanazawa-hakkei Station. They followed the Keikyu Line toward Yokohama for a good five minutes. When they reached the river, they followed that for another five.

The more time passed, the more residential the scenery got.

Fifteen minutes after leaving the college, they were lost in a sea of apartment buildings. Upscale exteriors could be seen in every direction. To Sakuta's eye, they looked rather European. And from the warmer end.

This neighborhood had a very different energy compared to the area around the station and college. If he'd been brought here blindfolded, there was a good chance he would've assumed himself in another country.

"You live around here?"

"……"

She pointedly ignored his question.

Their path took them through the complex. He wasn't sure this place was even open to the public. He was still worrying about that when Touko finally stopped.

They were at the corner of an apartment building, and it had a cake shop in the first-floor retail space.

Touko took a seat on the deserted patio.

"Mont Blanc and an Earl Grey," she said, looking at Sakuta.

He didn't want to annoy her, so he entered the shop and put in the order. This was proving to be a very expensive day. His wallet was almost empty.

He asked the staff to bring it to the patio and then went back outside.

Apparently, this place only pureed the chestnut cream to order. That explained why he hadn't seen any Mont Blancs sitting in the display case. But since this establishment was all about fresh ingredients, the finished cakes expired in two hours.

"You like Mont Blanc?" Sakuta asked, sitting down across from her.

"This place is especially good."

He'd half expected her to ignore him again, but this time he got an answer. Touko Kirishima *did* like Mont Blanc. This was not meaningful information, but Sakuta was one small step closer to learning who she was as a person.

At this point, the Mont Blanc arrived. It and the teacup were placed in front of Sakuta.

"You like Mont Blanc?" the waitress asked, setting down a fork next to it.

"I hear this place is especially good," he said.

Did he look like a boy with a sweet tooth visiting a cake shop alone? Probably.

She smiled at this, said, "Enjoy," and went back inside. Not once did she notice that Touko was seated across from him.

Proof again that only Sakuta could see her. That didn't change whether she was dressed as Santa or in ordinary clothes.

"Here," he said, sliding the cake across to her, along with the fork and tea.

Touko picked up the fork, placed her hands together, and whispered, "*Itadakimasu.*"

These habits persisted, even alone, even with no one watching. That's how natural the gesture came out.

And at last, it was time to Mont Blanc. Touko took a bite. The flavor immediately brought a smile to her lips, her whole face singing its praises.

"Anything else bothering you, Kirishima?"

"What do you mean, 'else'?"

"Anything you can't do without me around. Like order Mont Blanc here."

"……"

"This is Adolescence Syndrome, right?"

"Beyond the lack of Mont Blanc, I'm not especially bothered."

She sounded quite firm.

"Shopping?"

That had been an issue for Mai.

"You can buy anything online."

"But receiving the packages?"

You couldn't exactly sign for them while invisible.

"They have drop boxes, and these days, most places will just leave it at your door."

"……"

"Cat got your tongue?"

"Just feeling my dreams crumble. Santa shopping online, using drop boxes, getting packages piled up on your door."

"I think having the world made easy is a dream come true."

That interpretation did make a certain sort of sense. Perhaps to people from the olden days, they were now living in a world only dreamed up in novels and old movies.

"So you're satisfied with what you've got."

"I'm pretty far from 'satisfied.' I want my music reaching *way* more people."

Sakuta wasn't talking about her career. Touko knew that. She'd just said her piece anyway, deflecting from the topic at hand.

Formidable.

"You can do that even if you're visible."

"And I can do it even if I'm not."

Touko was *definitely* formidable.

"Any idea why you've ended up like this?"

With Mai, she'd had an extremely convincing reason why people had stopped perceiving her.

Everyone knew "Mai Sakurajima." She'd been acting since she was a little kid. Anytime, anywhere—there were eyes on her.

The entire student population at Minegahara had been unsure how to handle the celebrity in their midst.

In a sense, their goals had aligned.

The school had pretended not to notice Mai, and as they ceased to see her, they forgot she existed.

Touko was also not being seen or perceived, but the cause of Mai's case had been pretty specific. He couldn't just assume this case was triggered by something similar. The underlying circumstances didn't line up. The world knew all about Touko Kirishima and her music— but as an anonymous online singer. No one knew who she really was, what she looked like, how old she was, where she was from, her shoe size, or whether she liked Mont Blanc. There was no need to look away, no one unsure how to behave around her.

"But you had a problem that led to this."

She couldn't even order her own Mont Blanc and needed Sakuta to do that for her.

"You want to cure my Adolescence Syndrome, then?"

That wasn't an answer to his question, but it wasn't a denial, either.

"If you're deflecting this much, I take it you *do* know why."

She hadn't said she had no problems.

"Is this for me?" Touko asked. Again, not a denial. "Or for someone else?"

She was only answering with questions. Not changing her attitude one bit. Nothing he said rattled her or made her bat an eye.

It didn't seem like asking again would get him anywhere.

"For me, of course," he said. Following her lead seemed to be his only option. Maybe that would give him something to work with.

"I don't see how me being invisible has anything to do with you."

"I had one of those dreams. The ones that come true."

He wasn't sure when he'd received that present. It wasn't even obvious he had gotten a present until it became impossible to ignore. Sakuta only realized after a suspiciously realistic dream came true. Sara had become his student.

"If that dream is Adolescence Syndrome, it sounds like *you've* got the problem."

"I certainly do. I keep running into this Santa only I can see."

"Aha! In that case, curing my Adolescence Syndrome *would* benefit you."

Nothing she said offered any real information in it. The smell of the Mont Blanc was richer.

"You plan to keep doling out cases?"

He'd prefer those around him not start sprouting supernatural shit. Especially if that posed a threat to Mai; he *had* to put a stop to that.

"I'm releasing music. People who watch the videos are just responding to it. 'That's a good song!' 'It spoke to me!' 'It's like she's singing what I feel!' 'I want to hear more!' So I keep on singing."

She gave him a look that demanded to know what was wrong with that. Nothing was. Touko herself had committed no crime.

But it also wasn't something he could just let drop. She hadn't corrected him, either. The words she tossed out were hewing closer to the crux of the matter.

"So you're aware your music is triggering Adolescence Syndrome?"

"……"

Her fork paused inside the Mont Blanc.

That was why she'd said she let Uzuki read the room. It had reached her through a song. Spread via video-sharing sites.

That's how she'd given Adolescence Syndrome to ten million people. Looking at the replay numbers, that number was hardly exaggerated. If anything, it was evidence.

Sakuta was one of the people who clicked play.

"When's your next song coming out?" he asked.

Touko let out a little sigh.

"You calling me constantly is incredibly obnoxious, so I guess I can tell you."

She turned to him, brimming with confidence. She smiled, relishing this moment.

"I'm working on a new song. A Christmas number I want people hearing on the eve."

That obviously meant Christmas Eve. December 24. If Touko's songs had the power to trigger Adolescence Syndrome, then it was all too possible that it would kick off something. Or that song would make it more likely something might occur after that.

"So be a good boy and wait."

"Why—will something good happen?"

"Santa Claus's presents make everybody happy."

Touko did not sound like she was lying. Or like she was making fun of him. She genuinely thought releasing her new song would make everyone happy. She was certainly looking forward to it. But it didn't have any discernable connection to the threat against Mai. Or explain why he had to find Touko Kirishima.

"Everyone? Even that high school kid?"

He glanced across the lot, where a boy in uniform was parking a bicycle.

"If he's a good boy."

"And her?"

A college girl working in the shop was bringing coffee to a table.

"If she's a good girl."

"Then what about Mai?"

He was getting nowhere, so he threw out his girlfriend's name.

"……"

He felt the look in Touko's eyes shift momentarily. It was too brief for him to read any emotion in them. But there was no denying that Mai's name had provoked *some* sort of reaction.

"She doesn't need it. She's got everything."

Her tone hadn't changed. She was the same Touko he'd been talking to all along. Only the words had changed. He was pretty sure this was the first time she'd expressed a personal opinion about anyone other than Sakuta himself.

"Do you not like Mai?"

There'd been a hint of that behind her words.

"I used to have it in for her. Once."

Touko admitted it readily, but as a thing of the past.

"Not now?"

"She's dating this really weird dude, and I kind of admire that."

That was not necessarily a compliment. It was almost certainly half-sardonic. She was definitely mocking Sakuta himself, twisting the knife. But the "admire" part felt real to him. Authentic.

If he trusted that hunch, then Touko wasn't trying to harm Mai. That made things easier, but he still couldn't quite rule out the possibility, even if it seemed all too remote.

Seeking a more definitive answer, he probed deeper.

"Are you doing anything to Mai?"

He forced himself not to blink, watching closely.

And Touko's response was confusion.

"What are we talking about?" she asked, a beat later. It was a genuine question. Her head was slightly tilted as she looked him right in the eye, evidently thrown by his question.

"How much I love Mai," he said, looking away and leaning back in his chair. He was relieved. Her reaction suggested Touko herself was extremely unlikely to be the "danger."

"She really does have the oddest taste in boys. Strange, considering how she must have been spoiled for choice in her line of work."

Touko polished off the last bite of Mont Blanc, savored the flavor, then washed it down with the long-since-cold Earl Grey.

The empty cup landed on the saucer.

And Touko silently stood up.

This was an unmistakable signal their talk was over. But he couldn't just let her leave like this. He had to get enough to justify the expense of the cake and tea.

"Can I ask one last thing?"

"What?"

"How does it feel to have that many people hear your music?"

Sakuta stayed seated, peering up at Touko.

Singing—

—and having everyone hear her songs.

That was what mattered most to her right now.

What she'd said today made that clear to him and had prompted this question.

A genuine smile appeared on her lips. It was like she'd been waiting for him to ask.

"There's nothing like it. Nothing else feels this good."

She looked fulfilled. The light of accomplishment filled her eyes as she smiled at him from a place of sheer gratification.

A pure, innate emotion.

How could she stop doing something this fun? Why would she even consider it?

Her words, feelings, expression—it all spoke to how absorbed she was in her music.

"Thanks for this," Touko said. Like his final question had made her day. She waved once and walked merrily away. Sakuta sat watching until she was out of sight.

At last, the lights on the patio came on. Day had turned to night.

It was hard to put his feelings in words.

He'd learned about certain things. And grown more confused about others.

Urgency and understanding were all tangled up in Sakuta's mind.

But he felt like he'd gained one major hint.

Touko Kirishima's new song.

He'd have to be extra careful on Christmas Eve.

"If nothing else, I oughtta take some Mont Blanc home."

When he'd heard the bit about the two-hour time limit from the shopkeeper, he'd wanted to try it himself. He'd give this matter some more thought once he had some sugar in him.

It was Mai's birthday, and what better reason could there be to eat some cake?

6

With thirty minutes to spare on the Mont Blanc's life span, Sakuta finally reached Fujisawa.

He'd known two hours would be enough to make it home, but until the train actually pulled into the station, he'd felt like he was carrying a ticking time bomb. An extremely unnerving exercise.

What if the train ran late? What if an accident caused a delay?

Any problem could easily have delayed him until he ran out of time.

Fortunately, the train got him to Fujisawa right on schedule.

Now he just had to walk to his apartment on his own two feet. He went as fast as he could without jostling the cake box too much.

He made it home without incident. The Mont Blanc was safe and sound, and there was still time left before it expired. Relieved, he put his key in the door.

"I'm home," he called, and he took his first step in—and froze.

There were too many shoes. Girls' shoes.

Sakuta slipped his in at the end of the row and stepped up into the hall.

He could hear people moving but nobody talking. Only music, with a girl's voice singing.

He didn't know the song, but he knew the voice.

Up-tempo, sprightly rhythm, pleasant to the ear.

But the vocals and lyrics were forlorn, bittersweet.

Sakuta remembered what Touko had said to him.

"You're kidding…"

Was *this* her Christmas song?

He had to be sure, so he rushed into the living room.

"Sakuta, welcome back," Mai said. Of the four girls on the couch, only she turned to look at him. The others simply mouthed a greeting, their minds entirely on the TV screen. A cable ran to it from the laptop, the feed coming from a video-upload site.

Pure-white snow. Someone looking out of a room. A cat rubbing against their feet. No one else around. Someone lying on a bed, hands reaching up to the ceiling, grasping at something…but there was nothing there.

Where are you now? Who are you with? What's on your mind?
I'm alone at home. With my cat. Thinking of you.

*   *   *

But I'm not lonely. Not sad. The tears aren't flowing.
Not choking up, no pain in my heart, not suffocating.
So come on...

Let me know (I don't wanna know) who you love.
I have to know (I don't wanna know) about the one I love.

The visuals alone were nothing special.

But combined with these lyrics and vocals, they made it hard to breathe.

The song's name was "I Need You."

Release date—today. One hour before.

She'd mentioned Christmas Eve so he'd let his guard down.

Sakuta had assumed it wouldn't be *today.*

Touko Kirishima's name was right there in the uploader field.

Not long after, the song ended.

A momentary silence fell over the room.

Kaede reached for the laptop, lowered the volume, and hit play again. Then she finally said, "Welcome back, Sakuta."

"Yeah," he said, his eyes shifting to her side—where Nodoka and one other girl sat. "Why are you here, Zukki?"

He'd expected Mai and Nodoka, but Uzuki was a surprise. No wonder there'd been too many shoes at the door.

"I came to eat cake!"

There was a cake on the dining room table with several slices already missing.

"Wrong answer. You mean to celebrate Mai's birthday."

"I sang the song and everything!"

"Kaede and I sang with her," Nodoka added.

"Huh," he said, looking at his sister.

"Why wouldn't I?" she asked with a scowl.

"What's in the box?" Mai asked, glancing at his hand.

"Mont Blanc that only has fifteen minutes left to live."

Everyone had already eaten one slice of cake, yet Kaede, Nodoka, and Uzuki all wolfed down their share of Mont Blanc. This was a perfect example of the "sweets go in a second stomach" rule.

He'd only bought four of them, so he and Mai wound up splitting the last one. By the time they finished doing the dishes, it was almost eight.

"'Kay, I'm gonna walk Uzuki to the station."

"Zukki, you're not gonna spend the night at Mai's?"

"I'm heading to Hiroshima early tomorrow!" She grinned at him, flashing a peace sign. "Gotta get home and pack!" she added, following Nodoka to the door. Kaede tagged along and threw a coat on.

"I'll go with them part way. I wanna stop at the store."

"Okay, take care."

Sakuta finished drying his hands and poked his head around the table just in time to see Uzuki's hand waving one last time as the door clicked shut.

He went back to the living room.

"Kaede's being all considerate," Mai said.

It certainly didn't hurt to get a few extra minutes alone together on her birthday.

"Should we cuddle?"

"No."

"Aww."

"You met with her?"

That meant Touko Kirishima.

Mai's eyes were on the Mont Blanc cake box.

They'd just heard the Christmas song she'd said she was working on, which largely negated everything he'd felt like he'd gotten out of her.

Still, he relayed their conversation to Mai.

How she hadn't been a miniskirt Santa this time.

How she'd made him buy her Mont Blanc and tea.

That Touko knew her songs were causing Adolescence Syndrome.

And that she'd once had it in for Mai.

"What did you do?" he asked.

"Nothing. Never even met her."

"Do you get a lot of one-sided envy?"

Mai's status was rock-solid as an actress and a model. She'd gained fame as a kid and was popular with audiences from all walks of life. That meant there were also people who didn't care for her, who weren't happy about her success. Envy, jealousy, and inferiority were inescapable parts of the human experience.

"I do."

Mai nodded as if it were only natural. She was simply doing her best with the work she was given, but she was well aware that alone hurt people's feelings. Nodoka was only one person who'd wrestled with those emotions.

"But in your view, she's not specifically trying to harm me, right?"

"Right."

She definitely had thoughts on Mai. But he hadn't felt anything sinister enough to lead to crimes or accidents. The way she'd spoken about how she used to feel seemed more like how you avert your eyes from a bright light.

That meant they had to be on guard against the second possibility Rio mentioned.

The other main takeaway from his chat with Touko was the Christmas song. The one she'd wanted people to listen to the night before the big day. Perhaps she had further plans for Christmas Eve proper.

"Um, Sakuta…"

"Mm?"

"Don't make plans for the twenty-fourth or the twenty-fifth."

"I've kept them open so I can be with you, Mai."

"I don't want you fretting, so I'll be with you the whole time."

"Really?"

"Let's hit up a hot springs in Hakone and relax together."

"You're not gonna be all 'Sorry, work came in' on the day of, right?"

That had led to tears before.

"I've told Ryouko not to let that happen this time."

Still sounded risky.

"Toyohama and Kaede won't be with us?"

"Nodoka's got a Christmas concert, and Kaede's attending. Said she's gonna spend the holidays with your parents once that's over."

Sweet Bullet always had a Christmas concert lined up. Kaede had already told Sakuta she planned to go. Neither would be there to ruin his time with Mai.

"This is my Christmas present," Mai said. "Be there."

Naturally, Sakuta whooped it up.

And that very night...Sakuta Azusagawa had a strange dream.

Chapter
2
secrets and promises

1

December 24.

As Christmas Eve dawned, Sakuta was woken by Nasuno stepping on his face—just past eight, a little later than usual.

If he'd had classes, he definitely wouldn't have made it in time, but the last class on his schedule had been two days prior. He was free until the New Year and functionally already on winter vacation.

He could stay burrowed in his warm covers, sleeping in as much as he liked. It would've been fine to give in to the temptation. He didn't have any work plans, either. But he did have good reason to force himself out of his comfy bed.

"Freezing!"

He left his room, shivering.

In the living room, he fed Nasuno first. Dry cat food rattled into the bowl.

Then he put a slice of bread in the toaster and fried some sausages in the same pan as the eggs. A standard breakfast.

He and Nasuno ate together.

He did the dishes and started the laundry.

While he waited, he turned on the TV. He rarely watched it at this hour, so he wasn't really sure what was even on. He just flipped channels until Kaede stumbled blearily out of her room.

"Morning, Sakuta."

"Breakfast?"

"Yes, please."

Yawning, she sat down at the dining room table. He put a plate of precooked eggs and sausage before her.

"Can I get a cocoa?"

He put some in a panda mug, then topped it with the toast when it popped out before bringing both over to Kaede.

After she finished the eggs and sausage, she started tearing pieces off the toast and dunking them in the cocoa. She made it look delicious.

"What time you leaving?" he asked.

He'd heard she and her friend Kotomi Kano were going to see Sweet Bullet's Christmas concert today. After that, she'd be heading to their parents' place in Yokohama. They had a cake waiting for her.

"Just after ten. Gonna eat lunch with Komi. You?"

"Just past noon."

As he spoke, the laundry machine beeped.

"Tell Mom and Dad I'll pop by for New Year's," he said, heading for the laundry room.

"Will do," Kaede said through a mouthful of toast.

He hung up the laundry, vacuumed, saw Kaede out the door, and then started getting ready himself. Like he'd said, he left around noon.

"Nasuno, mind the fort."

Nasuno stopped washing her face and meowed back.

Sakuta headed to Fujisawa Station, a ten-minute walk from home. The heart of Kanagawa Prefecture's Fujisawa City, the JR, Odakyu, and Enoden Lines all ran through here.

He knew this station like the back of his hand, but today, it looked different. There were even more people flowing through.

Lots of them were carrying little gifts around, in addition to their standard backpacks or briefcases. A good number of them were dressed up in outfits they clearly didn't wear most of the time.

It was a very Christmas Eve crowd, and he watched it from the bridge leading to the station's north exit.

He stopped at the edge of the square just outside the electronics store. He could see many men and women meeting up here, and he was just one of them.

One after another, their partners arrived, and they vanished through the station gates. Hand in hand, arm in arm, or maintaining an awkward distance—but all enjoying the day in their own way.

The big clock in the square hit 12:29.

One minute till the time they'd agreed to meet.

As he watched that minute hand like a hawk, a voice came from behind him.

"I'm here!"

He turned slowly.

And found a girl a few years younger.

Sara Himeji.

She wore a chocolate-colored coat over a white sweater and a gray-checked miniskirt below that. Her healthy bare legs gleamed in the cold air. On her feet, she had short black boots. The outfit's colors were largely subdued, but the red scarf provided a Christmassy accent.

A man on his phone nearby did a very obvious double take. No doubt he thought she was cute.

"Opinions?" Sara asked, clearly looking for "Cute" or "Looks good."

"You look cold," Sakuta said, eyes on her legs. He felt significantly colder himself. A shiver ran down his spine.

"If you're gonna be mean, Teach, you choose my clothes."

Sara made a show of pouting, her eyes challenging him.

"Then I guess I'd better."

"Huh?"

"It's gonna get even colder later, so let's make a pit stop."

With that, he headed into the station building, searching for a clothing store.

"S-seriously?"

Sara had been joking, so she looked a bit rattled.

"If you're dress like that, you'll catch your death."

He meant that literally.

"That's not what I meant! You know that! You're so not fair."

He let her grumbling go in one ear and out the other as he hurried ahead.

They spent maybe half an hour shopping, and then Sakuta and Sara boarded the Enoden bound for Kamakura.

They found an empty seat and sat down together.

As the train pulled away, Sara stretched out her legs, scowling balefully at them. They were now covered in black skinny denim.

"Put those long legs away before someone trips," Sakuta said.

Sara wordlessly bent her knees.

"I spent a week picking that outfit out!" she said, sounding like she was making an announcement at a school board meeting.

"Perhaps you should have consulted the weather."

The train stopped at the next station, then slowly pulled out.

"I thought you were into bare legs and miniskirts, Teach."

"I am, but not if they give my students colds."

"I'd have been fine."

"Provide proof," he said, like an exam question.

"I am accustomed to wearing a school skirt that is even shorter," she said, intentionally sounding formal to match.

Her eyes were on a high school girl by the door—bare legs beneath a miniskirt.

"Isn't that cold?"

"Of course it is."

"I thought so."

Juri often had her tracksuit on underneath her skirt, but he'd never seen Sara do that. She was at the age when looking good mattered more than keeping warm.

The train stopped at Shichirigahama Station. The closest stop to Minegahara High—where Sara went and where Sakuta had gone. Several uniformed students disembarked. Judging from the oversize bags, they must have been on the volleyball team. Practice continued even on Christmas Eve.

The doors closed, and the train started moving.

It pulled slowly through the crossing and gradually rolled along to the next stop—Inamuragasaki Station. Here, it waited for a Fujisawa-bound train to pass before it started moving again.

From time to time, they caught glimpses of the sea between the buildings outside the windows.

That made it hard to tear his eyes away. But while he was waiting for the next peek, the train pulled into Gokurakuji Station. The temple of paradise—and the area was fittingly serene. Few people got off here.

"Teach, you remember our promise?"

Sara's voice broke the silence, her tone a striking departure from earlier.

"Hmm?"

"You promised not to cure my Adolescence Syndrome."

"I remember."

"But you're a liar," Sara said, grinning.

She held up her pinkie in front of him. Going for the pinkie promise.

"……"

Sakuta wordlessly wrapped his finger around hers as the doors closed. *"Pulling out,"* the announcement said, and the train lurched into motion. It soon grew dark—they'd entered a tunnel. This, between Gokurakuji and Hase Stations, was the sole tunnel on the Enoden Line.

With the lights gone, sounds echoed off the tunnel walls.

"The pinkie promise is as follows."

She chanted the words of the vow softly so only they could hear.

"Should I make these words a lie…"

The train moved on through the tunnel, headed for the light ahead.

"…a thousand needles will I swallow."

Almost at the exit.

"So this vow I can't deny."

Light returned to the carriage as Sara spoke the final phrase.

Their pinkies parted. Free of the tunnel, the car was bathed in light so bright he closed his eyes—and his vision *stayed* white. That seemed strange—but white noise filled his mind as well.

Something was definitely fishy here…and then Sakuta woke up.

The first thing he saw was his own pinkie, raised to make a promise. Then Nasuno, licking that finger. He could see a familiar white ceiling behind Nasuno's head. The same one he'd seen every morning since moving to Fujisawa.

"That was a dream…?"

He sat up, finding it hard to believe. His bed, the sheets, his desk, the curtains—all of them were telling him he was back in his own room.

The clock on his bedside table told him it was December 3.

"This is real, right?"

In lieu of an answer, Nasuno yawned.

2

"Azusagawa, finish bussing that and take your break."

Sakuta was carrying an empty cast-iron plate and rice bowl, and the manager was busy disinfecting the table behind him.

The lunchtime rush was nearly over, and seats were emptying.

"Will do," he said and took a step toward the back room.

"Oh, hold on…," his manager said, and he pulled up short.

"Need something?"

"Can you work Christmas? Twenty-fourth, twenty-fifth, either one!"

"Sorry, already made plans."

"Yeah, it *is* Christmas."

"Sorry again."

Sakuta bobbed his head, and this time he made his exit.

He left the dirty plates with the older lady on dishwashing duty, poured himself some tea from the staff pot, and stepped into the break room.

He put his cup down on the table. There was a sign taped to it that read CHRISTMAS BONUSES AVAILABLE! STAFF WANTED! Then in smaller writing, FREE CAKE! The manager's desperation was palpable.

"It is Christmas," he said, settling down on a folding chair.

What did the holidays have in store for him this year?

Until last night, he'd been looking forward to a blissful time with Mai.

But the dream he'd woken from this morning had completely dashed those hopes.

If that had been an ordinary dream, he'd have cheerily ignored it.

But since odds were high it was prophetic, he couldn't.

He'd dreamed Sara would become his student, and she had…and this dream felt the same. He'd only worked out that it was a dream after waking up.

But if this new dream actually happened, it would be a whole mess.

First—Sakuta was supposed to spend the twenty-fourth with Mai. He'd *just* agreed to go to Hakone with her the night before.

So why would he end up spending time with Sara Himeji? His brand-new student?

And one thing she'd said stuck with him.

——*"You promised not to cure my Adolescence Syndrome."*

He couldn't imagine why he'd agree to that. He certainly hadn't made any such promises yet. But the line did tell him one thing—

—Sara had Adolescence Syndrome.

She herself had admitted it.

"Oh brother."

The words slipped out of him.

"Senpai? What's up?"

To his surprise, someone answered. Tomoe had just emerged from the girls' locker room after changing into her waitress uniform.

"Had kind of a weird dream."

"Oh? You too?" she asked, blinking.

"Then you had one, Koga?"

Tomoe glanced at the clock on the time card machine. It was only 2:55, so she sat down across the table from him.

"Not me. Nana."

That would be her friend Nana Yoneyama.

"Said she had a super-realistic dream this morning."

Tomoe put her phone down on the table.

"What about?"

"Uh…I guess you're safe. I wanted to ask someone."

She seemed to have solved her own dilemma.

"I told you how Nana met her boyfriend?"

"Classmate from junior high, was it?"

"Yeah, but here's the thing…"

Tomoe trailed off, looking away uncomfortably.

"The thing?"

"The new dream was on Christmas Eve."

"Uh-huh."

Same day as his. Coincidence?

"And she and her boyfriend…were kissing."

The moment the words left her mouth, Tomoe gave him the sort of look you reserved for criminals.

"Kissing how?"

"How?!"

"Was she into it, or was he forcing it on her?"

That would make all the difference.

"Nana instigated."

"Good for her."

"So she came to me, going, 'What if this is a #dreaming thing and actually comes true—then what?'"

Tomoe clutched her phone as she squirmed.

"What do you think?"

"What's wrong with kissing?"

"She's an exam student! Is that allowed?"

Tomoe tapped her screen a few times, checking something. Probably scrolling through her chat history with Nana.

"I was making out with Mai all last year."

"Nana isn't like *you*."

"If she feels guilty about it, then just make up for it by studying harder."

In Sakuta's case, Mai had largely browbeaten him into applying himself. Like a hundred sticks to every carrot.

"I figured."

That had likely been Tomoe's gut response, but she hadn't wanted to give bad advice. She'd used Sakuta as a sanity check.

Her fingers were already tapping away.

"I'm guessing Yoneyama wants your approval."

"Don't spell it out, geez. Oh, she said, 'Thanks, I'll do that.'"

Did that mean study harder or go for the kiss? Probably both.

"People really buy into this hashtag thing, then?"

"I'm hearing more people talk about it at school."

"Huh."

That wasn't really a problem for him right now. But word of it spreading felt instinctively like bad news. The more convincing the stories got, the more people believed them, the less likely it was to fade out like the supernatural fad of the day.

If anyone saw a bad future in their dreams, they'd try to change it.

Right now, worrying about that was probably going too far. Overthinking things.

"So? What'd you dream about, Senpai?"

"I'm too ashamed to share after Yoneyama's slice of sweetness."

If he said he'd been on a date with Sara, there was no telling how Tomoe would react. The only thing he knew for sure was that there'd be a stream of invectives.

"Like you're even capable of shame."

She was already heaping on the abuse. Tomoe's eyes were back on the phone. A new message must have come in, because she was tapping away. Then she glanced up, giving him a dubious look.

"What did you do to Himeji?"

He hadn't expected that name from her. And that was a hot potato for him today.

"Nothing, yet. She just joined my class at the cram school."

This was true, so no reason to hide it. At the moment, they were nothing more than cram school teacher and student.

If that dream accurately predicted the future, then that might not last.

"Then why is she asking me for your contact info?"

Tomoe showed him her screen.

"Oh, 'cause I still haven't told her I don't own a phone."

"Can I tell her you're here working?"

"Yeah, sounds good."

With that, she turned her phone back around.

"When are you off?"

"Nine tonight."

"She's asking if you've got time after your shift."

Before he could answer…

"She'll be studying at the cram school till then," Tomoe said, reading.

"Got it."

Sakuta had business with Sara himself. About the dream and Adolescence Syndrome. Might as well take care of that today.

"'I'll be waiting for you, Teach!' she says."

Tomoe shot him a look, visibly displeased.

"What?"

"Nothing!"

She made that sound like it was totally something, but she got up to start her shift.

"Himeji's just a real heartbreaker. Better watch yourself, Senpai."

Tomoe was out the door before he could ask why.

3

When work ended, Sakuta left the restaurant. It was 9:05. Not wanting to keep Sara waiting, he'd punched out at nine on the dot. He'd changed, said bye to everyone else working, and been out the door.

He headed toward the station, down a road covered in Christmas decor. He soon heard footsteps coming up behind him. Just as he started to wonder, someone threw their arms around him. Gloved hands covered his eyes.

"Guess who!"

Who did he know who'd pull a prank like this? The first person who popped into his mind was currently in far-off Okinawa. And if it were her, the voice alone would have given her away.

After a moment's thought, he found the answer.

"Study-slacking Himeji."

"*Bzzt*, incorrect."

She sounded put out. The hands left his eyes and her weight no longer pressed on his back. She circled around to stand in front of him.

"The correct answer is that it's me, just taking a breather."

Sara smiled, happy her prank had been a success.

"So you do have a childish side, then."

She seemed more levelheaded than most people her age. His impression of her was that she was collected and mature, so this came as a surprise.

"I *am* still a child, you know? Three years younger than you, Teach."

She held up three gloved fingers.

"I feel like saying you're a child proves you aren't."

At the very least, the way Sara used it proved she knew how to use that word to her advantage.

"But do you actually think I'm a grown-up?"

"The word I'd go for is *adolescent*."

He chose that word intentionally, going for a light jab. If his dream was right, and she had Adolescence Syndrome...and knew she did, then he'd hoped he might get a reaction from her.

But Sara didn't bat an eye.

"That's definitely accurate."

She just caught the ball and ran with it. No signs of raised hackles. No surprise, trepidation, or unease. Just a pleasant smile, beaming back at him. This told him nothing. He'd have to find another angle.

"Oh, I left my bag in the study room."

"Then let's head back there. It's cold out."

"True!"

It might have been half past nine, but the cram school interior was still brightly lit. Unthinkable at regular schools, but normal here. Still, it was Saturday, so there were fewer people actually hanging out.

"Anyone in the classrooms?"

"Classes have all wrapped up."

"I'll grab my bag, so wait for me there."

Sara vanished into the self-study booth, so Sakuta headed on to the classroom, the smallish cubicle he always taught in. With only a table and a whiteboard, it seemed hardly worth calling a "classroom."

He was still standing by the whiteboard when Sara caught up, bag in hand.

She smoothly pulled out a chair and took a seat. Both had assumed positions like class was in session. The only difference was the lack of textbook, notes, and writing implements in front of her.

"Kind of exciting having no one else here," she said, leaning across the table, one hand by her mouth to project the whisper.

During regular hours, this place was filled with the murmur of students asking questions and teachers explaining things. Having none of that felt novel to Sakuta, too.

"Any problems you didn't get on finals?"

Sakuta taught math, and that exam was on the first day—yesterday.

"Totally nailed it. Your exam strat worked like a charm, Teach."

"Let's hope it worked for Yamada, then."

"If he's lucky!"

She was in his class, and her laugh suggested she knew better. He must have sounded pretty hopeless after the exam. Kento was totally that type. Sadly, it was far too easy to picture.

"Well, if this isn't about the exam, then…?"

He put the query in a look. Sara caught his gaze and held it.

"Teach…you know about the dreaming hashtag?"

"Been hearing that term a lot, yeah."

He'd just talked to Tomoe about it earlier.

"Well, I had a strange dream this morning."

"Uh-huh. And you think it's related?"

He had not prepared for this eventuality. But in hindsight, it did seem like a reasonable one.

"It took place on Christmas Eve…"

"Mm-hmm."

"And I was with you."

"……"

"I think we were on a date."

So far, it matched his dream exactly.

"Were we making a pinkie promise on the Enoden?"

"Huh…?"

"Just past Gokurakuji Station."

"What?!"

Sara was totally reeling.

"……Teach, you mean…?"

Sakuta answered in the affirmative.

"Probably the same dream."

"Is that even possible?!"

Sara sounded thrilled. Curiosity defeated surprise or unease.

"I guess so. It happened to us."

If the dreams came from things that *would* take place, it made sense that the people involved in that future event would both have the same dream. It wouldn't add up if one of them was off on their own, doing something else when the day came around.

And if this dream showed Sakuta and Sara's future, he had some questions.

"Just to be clear…"

"The Adolescence Syndrome thing?"

This time she got ahead of him.

"Yeah. That true? You said I'd promised not to cure you."

"Totally true. I *do* have Adolescence Syndrome."

Sara's smile was open, the admission ready. No trace of guilt or hesitance. It didn't seem like she was the least bit put out by it. Like he'd asked if she could play piano and she'd simply said yes.

"What kind?" he asked.

"That's a secret!"

The exact same tone, but this time she wasn't answering.

"Since when?"

"The first day of Golden Week."

That she was willing to answer. And with immense precision. It was December now, so she'd been like this the better part of a year. If she still knew the exact date, something pretty memorable must have happened.

"Did you have a real bad day?"

"Got my heart broken."

Again Sara answered, but with no signs of lingering grief.

"But not like a boyfriend dumped me or I asked someone out and got rejected," she added, before he could say anything else.

"Then it must've been the other cliché. You found out the person you liked was in love with someone else."

"Please don't make it sound so predictable."

The implication must have rankled. She half blushed and pouted.

"But it doesn't seem like it bothers you anymore."

"Nope! I'm over it."

She appeared to be telling the truth. Nothing seemed forced. Sara was just speaking her mind.

"Adolescence Syndrome got me through it."

He was fairly confident she meant every word and believed what she was saying.

But that's what bothered Sakuta. Sara herself was totally convinced she'd gotten over it, so why was her Adolescence Syndrome ongoing? That didn't add up.

"Every day is a blast now. I know I said it in the dream, but, Teach— please don't cure my Adolescence Syndrome."

"Do I look like a doctor specializing in weirdo diseases?"

"Not at all."

Sara laughed out loud.

"Why do you think I said that?"

"Beats me."

"Oh, and can we keep this just between the two of us?" she added, as if it just occurred to her.

"This?"

"You know. Don't make me spell it out. My Adolescence Syndrome, obviously."

"I won't tell anyone."

"Really?"

Her smile faded, and she gave him a look.

"Even if I did, no one would believe me. They'd just think I was crazy."

Sakuta gave her a reason to believe, and Sara smiled again.

"True," she said.

"And if I don't even know what kind of Adolescence Syndrome it is, I can't exactly make a good story out of it."

This was his roundabout way of posing the question again.

"You're that curious?"

She'd undoubtedly caught his drift.

"Well, if it doesn't hurt me, I'm not that interested."

If pushing didn't work, then maybe pulling would.

"You should care more about your students, Teach."

"Will that make you tell me?"

"Let's make it a homework assignment. You have to figure out what my Adolescence Syndrome is."

"Always hated homework."

"Turn it in once exams are over."

"Is there a reward if I do?"

"Let me think," Sara said, making a pensive face. Then she smiled. "If you get it right, I'll do any one favor you ask."

"Sounds like fun."

"Obviously, no *sexual* favors."

She laughed out loud but was interrupted when the phone in her bag vibrated.

"Oh, that time already?"

The clock showed it was almost ten.

"Mom's picking me up at the station, so I gotta run."

Sara hopped up and shouldered her bag, putting the phone to her ear.

"Oh, Mom, sorry! Still inside. Be right there!"

With that, she hung up. On her way out of the cubicle, she turned back one last time.

"Don't forget your homework!" she said with a breezy smile.

Sakuta made a face, which seemed to please her, and she trotted off down the corridor.

"No running in the halls!" he called, but she was out of sight before he finished.

"......"

He was left alone in the deserted school.

"Well, that was a weird turn."

Rather than making progress, he'd wound up with more problems. Where was this all headed? He couldn't begin to guess.

"......Well, I'd better go home."

Sitting here wouldn't resolve anything. That alone was certain.

He headed down the corridor Sara had taken, back to the faculty area. There were still teachers at work beyond that counter.

Not wanting to interrupt them, he kept the obligatory good-byes barely audible—a token nod to manners—and left the school.

He pressed the button for the elevator. It was already on its way up, so it reached the fifth floor in less than ten seconds. A soft *ding*, and the doors opened.

"?!"

He heard a gulp of surprise from within.

He'd assumed there was no one on board, but he was proved wrong. And he knew who—that question was resolved instantly.

"'Sup, Futaba."

Rio stepped off the elevator.

"I…forgot something yesterday," she said. Excuses.

"That's not like you," he said. Even weirder that she'd come to get it at this hour.

"Why are *you* here, Azusagawa?"

"Should I not be?"

Rio's tone was positively accusatory.

"Something came up. But, uh, I am glad to run into you. Wanted to pick your brain—you free after this?"

It was pretty late, but if he'd caught her, that worked for him.

"Just give me a minute. I…I probably need your advice, too."

That was not a line he heard from her every day.

Rio soon came back from the locker room, now carrying a gray coat.

"That's what you forgot?"

"Come on!" she said, ignoring him and stepping onto the elevator.

But leaving without your coat at this time of year took some doing. Something unprecedented must have gone down the day before.

Which was probably why Rio needed advice.

Outside, they headed south toward the station and turned in to a hamburger joint just down the Enoden tracks. This place had a liquor license, and a couple of large parties were already yukking it up.

Sakuta was hungry, so he placed an order. Not long after, they brought out a hefty-sized burger on a plate. Rio had ordered nothing besides a caffe latte, but he paid that no heed and took a big bite. The look in her eyes clearly communicated "That many calories, at this hour? Seriously?"

When he finished his burger, he started picking at his fries and filling her in on the day's twists.

The dream he'd had.

How he'd been with Sara.

How she'd mentioned Adolescence Syndrome.

And then how he'd met up with her just now and verified that fact.

When he was done, Rio sighed.

"And you've already broken your promise and told me."

"Well, apparently, I'm a liar."

"I knew that."

"What do you make of it?"

"Well, your dream at least clarifies the threat to Sakurajima."

"Does it?"

He had no clue what Rio meant.

"You cheating on her is as good as stabbing her in the back."

"……I suppose that would count as 'Mai's in danger.'"

But it didn't connect to "Find Touko Kirishima."

"Jokes aside…"

"With you, it might not be a joke." Rio sounded like she meant this.

"You think I'd cancel an all-night date with Mai to go out with Himeji?"

"Not if it was just an ordinary date, no."

"See?"

"But I bet that changes if you've got a lead on curing her Adolescence Syndrome."

"If Himeji's Adolescence Syndrome puts Mai in danger, then yeah."

If that was the deal, he'd *have* to cancel their plans. Or preferably, postpone them.

"I feel like you'd go even if Sakurajima wasn't involved."

"If no harm, no foul. I might ignore it completely. She doesn't even want to be cured."

If Sara wanted to keep things the way they were, who was he to argue?

"Then you'll just have to do this homework and work out if her Adolescence Syndrome is harmful or not. As long as there's the slightest chance it's related to that warning."

"I guess."

That would let him figure out his next move. Finishing that homework was the only way to know for sure.

"Homework. Ugh," he grumbled.

The worst part was he had no clues to work with. All Sara had admitted was that heartbreak had triggered it and this had occurred during Golden Week.

He'd need a better hint than that before he could even start brainstorming.

"If you don't want to solve the problem yourself, just cheat," Rio said. How inappropriate.

"Cheat how?"

Sakuta was all in favor of that. The rules here were hazy, and no one would question his approach.

"Sara Himeji isn't the only one who might know the answer here," Rio said.

That got him there. "...Oh, Touko Kirishima?"

If Sara's Adolescence Syndrome was a gift from Touko, then there was a chance she'd know the specifics. Touko had known exactly what was going on with both Uzuki and Ikumi.

"Guess I'll just have to meet her again."

Either way, he still had loads of questions for her.

Curing Touko's Adolescence Syndrome might well be the most urgent task on his list. And meeting her in person was the fastest, surest means of finding a clue on how to do that.

That was likely a shortcut to solving Sara's homework, too.

"Glad I talked to you, Futaba. Thanks."

"You're welcome."

She grabbed a single fry and ate it, like that was her fee. Sakuta waited till she swallowed, then changed the subject.

"So what advice did you want?"

"Well…"

Rio's gaze dropped, and she studied the foam on the latte.

"……"

"……"

He waited, but no further words emerged.

Was it really that hard to talk about?

"What, did someone ask you out?"

"?!"

Sakuta had just been trying to loosen her lips, but Rio's reaction was all too obvious. He might have hit the jackpot.

"……Seriously?" he asked.

Rio managed a very small nod.

"Who?"

"One of my…"

"Oh, Toranosuke Kasai?"

"……How did you figure that out?!"

Rio glared up at him through her lashes. With her face that red, it was not the least bit intimidating.

"Well, he's been radiating a love aura for ages."

"…And you didn't tell me?!"

Her glare grew baleful.

"I thought it would be funnier… No, that's not true. It's just not fair to go behind the kid's back."

"……"

Her silence signaled resentment. But Sakuta was pretty sure he had the moral high ground here. It wasn't right to blab other people's feelings.

"When was this?" he asked.

"Yesterday," she said, hands clutching her latte cup.

"Where?"

"My classroom at the cram school."

"How'd he bring it up?"

"He'd been having trouble focusing on the lessons lately, and I wondered if something was on his mind, but when I asked…"

"That's totally your fault."

"I wouldn't have if you'd warned me!"

"So what'd you say?"

"Before I said anything, he said he didn't need an answer and left."

"Aha."

Probably couldn't handle the embarrassment. He'd seen the boy with Rio before, and just standing next to her had left him in a tizzy.

"What should I do?"

"Whatever you want to do, Futaba."

"I've never even thought about it."

"Then here's your chance."

"I hate it when you're right."

"I think this is a good opportunity for you."

He took a sip of the coffee he'd ordered with the burger.

"Opportunity for what?"

"I don't think dragging Kunimi around forever is good for you."

"I'm not."

"Reaaaally? Aren't you still comparing every other guy to him?"

"……No."

She might deny it, but her body language was not convincing anyone. She likely wasn't *consciously* making those comparisons; in all likelihood, she'd only just realized when he pointed it out, which explained her reaction.

"Don't do that. You're never gonna find anyone better than Kunimi. His sole flaw is his taste in women."

"Kunimi's girlfriend is a perfectly fine individual."

"Is she?"

"Kunimi's mother works at a hospital, right? She heard about that and decided to become a nurse herself."

"How do *you* know this, Futaba?"

"Before we graduated, I asked him what he liked about her, and that's what he told me."

"......What a terrifying question."

Bad for the heart. Even hearing it secondhand, well after the fact, Sakuta was ready to suffocate. He almost went blue in the face.

"But wait, does that mean you knew? That Kamisato was in the nursing school at my college?"

"I knew that, yeah."

Neither Yuuma nor Rio had breathed a word about it. Six whole months had passed in blissful ignorance before he ran into her at a mixer, of all godforsaken places.

That had nearly killed him, and he could have used a warning.

"We *are* friends, right?"

"Some things you can't tell your friends."

That phrase clearly didn't apply here. He would die on that hill.

Rio swiped another fry. She cleaned her fingers and said, "But, uh...thanks."

"Mm?"

"Talking about it has helped me collect myself."

"I will hear you out on anything this funny."

"I'm definitely asking someone else next time."

Rio drained the rest of her latte. The clock had hit eleven thirty, and the shop was ready to close.

4

He spent the weekend working and, by Monday, was back on the usual college grind.

Each day, he looked for Touko on the gingko lane as he headed to his classes.

And between classes, on his way to lunch, and the way out—always scanning the student throngs for a miniskirt Santa. But ever since he bought her a Mont Blanc, he hadn't seen Touko on campus once.

He also called her daily. Kaede gave him some withering looks, but he left messages on her voice mail anyway. Touko didn't pick up or call back once.

A week went by without any progress, and before he knew it—it was Friday.

December 9.

He was packing up his empty lunch when Takumi growled, "There's more every day," his eyes on the view outside the window.

"More what?" he asked, joining Takumi at the window.

"Couples."

They were on the third floor and had a good view of the path below. It was not hard to spot a number of couples walking very close together. Heads thrown back, laughing at each other's jokes.

"This is their season," Takumi grumbled. He seemed extra bitter. "One big day after another."

"Are there that many?"

"Christmas Eve? Christmas?"

"Those are usually treated as a single occasion."

"New Year's Eve? New Year's Day?"

"Are those for couples?"

"What, you aren't going to spend them with Sakurajima?"

"Of course I am."

If Mai's schedule allowed it, at least.

"See? They're for couples. All that happiness has rotted your brain, Azusagawa."

Vicious.

"And after New Year's, you've got Setsubun? Valentine's? White Day?"

One of those definitely didn't fit, but Sakuta opted to not point that out. They were all a long ways off.

"Christmas comes before anything next year."

And that was the one holiday on Sakuta's mind. Would he be able to keep his word and spend it with Mai? Or would he wind up with Sara, like the dream said?

"Exactly! Gotta get a girlfriend first. That's why I'm setting up a mixer. Once it's set, you gotta be there, Azusagawa."

"Ew, no. I've gained nothing from that experience."

His first-ever mixer had been rendered extremely uncomfortable by the arrival of the last person he expected. He would likely never fully recover from it. The painful memories had been seared into his mind.

"See, another couple!"

Takumi pointed through the window. A man and woman, goofing around. The girl was pushing the guy forward. Why was that so much fun? Who knew, but they were sure laughing.

"Love blinds them all," Takumi whispered distantly.

Eyes on the window, Sakuta failed to respond. His mind was elsewhere—he'd caught a glimpse of red down the lane.

A miniskirt Santa.

That was definitely Touko Kirishima's back.

Leaving his bags where they were, Sakuta rushed to the door.

"What? Huh? Class is starting!"

"Tell 'em I'm in the can!"

He was gone.

"Ew, I don't wanna."

By the time Takumi's voice reached his ears, Sakuta was already on the stairs.

*　　*　　*

As he left the building, the bell rang, signaling the start of class.

Moving against the last few stragglers, he headed toward the tree-lined lane.

And he stopped near the main gates.

The lady he was after was not ten yards out.

Touko was standing her phone upright on a bench, walking a few paces down the lane, then coming back to check the phone.

What was she up to?

The results must not have been satisfactory, because she put the phone back down and repeated the walk. The way she walked seemed theatrical, like a model on a runway.

Sakuta approached, calling out.

"Um…"

"Don't come this way. You'll ruin the shot."

"Huh?"

Touko turned to face him, looking annoyed. He thought she was coming to him, but she brushed right past and reached for the phone.

"What are you doing?"

"Filming a video from the Christmas song."

"Didn't you put that out? The day of the Mont Blanc."

"That was a different song."

She didn't even glance his way, just put her phone back on the bench. But it fell over the second she let go.

"Need a hand?"

"……"

"I mean, it seems like this isn't working."

"Then follow and film me."

Touko held out the phone. The recorder was already open.

"Press the red dot to record."

With that, Touko started walking off down the lane. Sakuta trailed behind, keeping her back in frame.

Fortunately, with class in session, there were few students here, and no one was giving him funny looks. The few people they did pass didn't seem to think he was doing anything weird. Maybe walking around filming things was normal now.

"Is talking allowed?" he asked when he was sure no one was in earshot.

"I'm only using the video, so we can—just try not to be a headache."

"Can I ask about Sara Himeji's Adolescence Syndrome?"

He figured the direct approach would be less of a pain.

"Who's that?" Touko asked. Not helpful.

"Student of mine."

"Why would I know?"

"She said she'd got Adolescence Syndrome."

"And?"

"If that's a present from you, I figured you might know more."

"I don't."

With that, she stopped and turned to face him. Heels clicking, she stalked over and snatched the phone away.

"If she's got it, I'm pretty sure I gave it to her, though."

She was already checking the video he'd taken.

A long shot of a miniskirt Santa walking away. He could hear their dialogue playing back, too. And Touko insisting she'd never heard of Sara.

"You knew Hirokawa and Akagi."

"Well, they're students here."

She seemed irked he'd ask something that obvious. Didn't seem like she was lying or deliberately messing with him. She was just stating the facts. And mildly exasperated, apparently.

"So much for cheating."

This left him with no way of finding out what Sara's Adolescence Syndrome was. He'd just have to wait for something weird to happen.

He wouldn't know until it affected him. He'd rather stay well clear of that, but…he didn't see any other way to progress.

"Thanks, this should work nicely," Touko said, nodding. She'd clearly gained more from this than he had.

"Feel free to call me anytime you need a cameraman."

"Yeah? Then come here on the twenty-fourth. I'm doing a live stream. See you here at four."

"Uh, that day won't really work…"

"Be there."

Not listening to his protests, Touko headed off to the main gate. He watched her cross the campus and vanish from view.

"Christmas Eve was bad enough already."

He already had the problem posed by that weird dream, and now she was dropping another deal on top of that. How was he supposed to tell Mai about all this?

"……Guess I'd better get to class."

Taking too long in the bathroom would cause his teacher unnecessary concern.

5

The next day was December 10, a Saturday.

He spent the morning cleaning and doing laundry. Then he gave Nasuno a bath. Mai came over for lunch, and they cooked and ate together.

She had a magazine interview that afternoon, so he saw her off and left the house himself just past four. He was teaching at the cram school at six.

He'd left early because he was champing at the bit, for obvious reasons. Sara's homework.

It was due today, but all he had was a blank sheet of paper.

Leaving the house wouldn't help with that, but Nasuno seemed disinclined to provide any answers. At the very least, he hoped moving around would help him feel less stir-crazy.

Even if he arrived at work early, he could at least do class prep.

Maybe an idea would hit him on the walk in.

That was but a faint hope, and he arrived at Fujisawa Station no closer to figuring out the nature of Sara's Adolescence Syndrome. He definitely needed a hint.

He dragged his feet up onto the pedestrian overpass—and a voice called out from behind him.

"Um, Azusagawa-sensei."

A male voice.

That alone didn't bring a face to mind.

Wondering who it was, Sakuta turned around—to find himself staring at a wall. A wall made of a Minegahara uniform and a large bag stuffed with a basketball uniform. Toranosuke Kasai stared down at Sakuta from a height of nearly six foot three.

"Sorry to bother you."

"What's this about?"

"Do you have a moment to chat?"

"Sure, but…me?"

He'd had no contact with the boy before.

"Yeah."

"Not Futaba?"

"You, Azusagawa-sensei," Toranosuke said, almost on top of him.

"Then…in the cram school?"

"Er, no, I'd rather not…"

The boy's gaze wandered. Sounded like he didn't want anyone to hear this.

"Then somewhere closer."

Since Sakuta was here early, he had time to talk.

They wound up sitting in the restaurant Sakuta also worked at. This earned them a look from the waitress—Tomoe—but she also seated them in back, ideal for hushed voices.

Each ordered drinks only and settled down across from each other, armed with coffee and cola, respectively.

"So what's on your mind?" Sakuta asked, pretty sure it would be Rio. That was the only topic they really had in common.

But Toranosuke brought up a different name.

"I think you oughtta keep an eye on Sara—I mean, Himeji."

A bolt from the blue, it took him a moment to catch up. Why'd he call her by her first name, then correct himself? Careful about what? Questions streamed past him.

"How so?"

He was clueless, so he decided to go one step at a time.

"You're Sara's third teacher, Azusagawa-sensei. Himeji's, I mean."

"At this point, just use her first name."

"Fair."

Toranosuke nodded readily. Anyone could tell he was a pretty serious kid.

"I'm aware of what happened with her previous teacher," Sakuta said.

Sakuta worked here part-time, but that teacher had been full-time, in his late twenties.

"And you know why she's not his student anymore?"

"Basically, yeah."

Bluntly speaking, he'd tried to hit on a student, and that obviously hadn't turned out so well.

"Sara's first teacher got replaced for the exact same reason."

This was news to him.

"He also fell for her?"

"……"

A silent nod.

"I've heard any number of kids at school have asked her out, too."

"She does seem the type."

Breezy, well-mannered, straight-A student. Someone who smiled a lot and brightened every room she entered. She wasn't the least bit shy, either. More than just approachable, Sara actively reached out to others.

It felt entirely natural all the boys would fall for her. Sakuta's class was no exception—Kento was yet another of her conquests.

"If you're worried about the attention she gets, look out for her yourself, Kasai. You're on a first-name basis, right?"

"It can't be me," Toranosuke said firmly.

"Why not?"

"She lives next door…"

"How's that a problem?"

It didn't seem like an issue, but Toranosuke wasn't done.

"Our parents are close, so we grew up playing together."

"Childhood friends?"

"Basically."

He didn't sound too concerned about what to call it. Perhaps their relationship was such a constant in his life that he never bothered thinking about concrete definitions.

"And…until junior high, I thought I loved her."

Suddenly, romance entered the conversation.

"We were always together, and everyone teased us about looking like a couple…"

"That happens, yeah."

Probably out of envy.

"It didn't seem like the worst idea, and I assumed eventually we would end up together."

"But you didn't."

Sakuta knew perfectly well that Toranosuke was now asking Rio out.

"Yeah. One day, I realized what I thought was love didn't even come close to the real thing."

"When you fell for Futaba?"

"Yeah."

The truth came out before he could second-guess his answer.

"……"

"……"

"Huh?!"

There was a very long pause before he looked shook. He jaw dropped, and his lips flapped as he searched for words and found none. He settled for letting his eyes swim. Trying to cover the awkwardness, Toranosuke took a sip of cola, but he messed up and wound up coughing.

"H-how?" he managed at length. It had been a full thirty seconds after Sakuta had dropped that on him.

"I saw you at school, practically glowing while you asked her questions."

"……"

Another long silence followed. The boy looked like he was on the verge of clutching his head.

"She's a tough nut to crack, but good luck."

"Th-thanks… Wait, no, that's not the point!"

His bulky frame all hunched up, Toranosuke attempted to get the conversation back on track.

"So what are Himeji's feelings for you?" Sakuta asked.

"I believe they were favorable."

"Past tense."

"I'm not sure about now."

Fair enough. He wasn't her. Sara's feelings were hers alone. And if she herself wasn't fully aware of them, how could anyone else be? Like Toranosuke himself, before he met Rio. It didn't take much to provoke confusion, misunderstanding, or self-deception. And it was hard for anyone to extract themselves from that.

"To your eyes, what sort of girl is Himeji?"

"Meaning…?"

"Cheery? Well-mannered but in a relatable way? Has she always been like that?"

"Yeah. Ever since kindergarten. Always at the center of the crowd, smiling. Everyone flocks to her."

"Same in grade school?"

"Yep."

"And junior high?"

"Yep."

"On top of which, they thought you two were dating."

"……"

It sounded like the perfect life. She'd probably never experienced any real setbacks until Toranosuke effectively dumped her.

Which likely meant it had been a real blow. Shocking enough to cause Adolescence Syndrome. Things were adding up, but it also felt a bit too simplistic.

"Long story short, you dumped her…"

"I didn't do that."

"Functionally speaking. But once you two were through, she got real popular, and that worries you?"

"Yeah. So I'd like you to keep an eye on her."

"But why come to me?"

Sakuta and Toranosuke hadn't really spoken before. There had to be some reason why he'd suddenly broach a subject like this.

"I hit up Kunimi-senpai for advice yesterday, and he said to go to you."

"That guy always has to stick his nose in."

"And also…you're not like her previous teachers. You've already got a great girlfriend."

"True…"

That kind of made sense, but it also felt a bit off base. At the very least, he got why Toranosuke would assume anyone dating Mai Saku-rajima wouldn't accidentally fall for Sara.

"Please, Azusagawa-sensei."

Toranosuke bowed his head.

Keeping tabs on a girl too popular for her own good was hardly Sakuta's territory. It wasn't a problem a part-time cram school teacher should be worrying about at all.

"I just teach math."

But Toranosuke was serious, and Sakuta couldn't exactly ignore his request. He had the dual obligations of someone older and a teacher, even if only in name.

Most of all—Sara *was* his student. The shared dream had given them an odd connection. She'd assigned him a tough assignment to figure out her Adolescence Syndrome, so arguably he was already keeping an eye on her.

And what Toranosuke had told him might well have something to do with her symptoms. It certainly seemed worth considering.

"Okay, then. I'll keep an eye on her."

Only then did Toranosuke finally raise his head.

"Thank you."

He looked relieved in a way that betrayed his youth. And the fact that he could recognize that was a powerful reminder for Sakuta that he himself was no longer in high school.

They settled the tab and left the restaurant just past five thirty.

While they'd been talking, the sun had gone down, and the street-lights flickered on.

Toranosuke had a class to attend, so they walked toward the office building that housed the cram school.

Their conversation had taken up the time Sakuta had originally intended to devote to Sara's homework, but it had given him some unexpected insights.

Given what each had told him, Toranosuke was likely the boy who'd broken her heart without her ever telling him how she felt.

And after that—she got very popular.

He couldn't tell if that romantic interest was the result of Adolescence Syndrome or not. He'd never encountered any symptoms that could cause that. But the timing made it hard to rule out completely. Unless his lack of other clues just made him want to connect the two.

Rationally speaking, there was every chance the two were unrelated.

With Toranosuke out of the picture, the boys who'd long nursed crushes on her might have stopped keeping it to themselves. It could easily be as simple as that.

Sakuta was no closer to an answer to the homework assignment. But thanks to Toranosuke, he wasn't entirely empty-handed.

"You got Futaba's class today?"

Toranosuke looked pretty stressed out. Since they'd left the restaurant, his movements had been so stiff Sakuta could almost hear the joints creaking. Every part of him radiated tension.

"Yes, but that's settled."

"How so?"

"I…had a dream."

"A dream."

"One where she rejected me on Christmas Eve."

"Uh-huh."

That didn't seem like a coincidence. This was the third Christmas Eve dream. Sakuta and Sara's, Nana's dream Tomoe had told him about, and now Toranosuke's.

"You've heard of the #dreaming thing?"

"What did Futaba say, exactly? In the dream?"

"Mm? Uh…'I can't date a student.'"

"So you're gonna give up?"

"Honestly, I'm not sure what to do. Even after that dream…I still can't get her out of my head. But I knew it probably wouldn't pan out from the get-go, so…I dunno what to say."

His line of thought petered out, and he wound up apologizing.

Earnest, honest, awkward, and unsteady. The sincerity was almost uncomfortable to watch. But it also made Sakuta want to offer more.

"If it were me, I'd say, 'If I pass the exams at my first-choice college, go out with me then.'"

Toranosuke was still in his second year. He had a full year to persevere.

"……"

The advice seemed to stun him. Like he still hadn't processed the meaning.

"That is, if you're serious about her."

"I—I am. I'll give it a shot…!"

His mind caught up, and his voice squeaked, a mixture of panic and glee.

"And if you don't want her grumbling at you, hit the books."

"Yeah, of course. Uh, Azusagawa-sensei, seriously…"

Toranosuke turned to thank him but then flinched instead. His eyes flicked past Sakuta's shoulder, to where the station lay.

"Sorry, I gotta run," he blurted, and he dashed off toward the school.

A moment later…

"Azusagawa?" a voice behind.

"'Sup, Futaba."

Rio had been coming their way.

That explained why Toranosuke had fled the scene. He would have to sit through class with her later, so this was not a promising sign.

"Was that Kasai with you?"

Anyone as tall as that boy stood out in a crowd. Even from a distance, she'd have recognized him.

"They're childhood friends."

"Who and who?" Rio asked, lost.

"Kasai and Himeji. He shared a few things."

"Was that all?"

"That's all."

"......You didn't say anything unnecessary?"

She was already giving him a reproachful look.

"Only what I deemed *necessary*."

"That's probably what I'm talking about."

Clearly, Rio wasn't done complaining at him. But before she could say anything else, a new voice interrupted them.

"Teach!"

Bright and bouncy.

Sara came running over from the station.

Beaming all the while like she was having the time of her life.

"Look at this!"

She reached into her bag, pulled out a folded sheet of paper, and spread it out to show him.

It was an answer sheet covered in circles indicating correct answers. Not a single response was crossed out. Full marks.

"Oh dear," he said. "We're supposed to be reviewing the answers you got wrong today."

Without mistakes, there was nothing to be done.

"Praise comes first!"

"Well done."

"I'll go on ahead," Rio said and headed inside.

"I'm coming, too!" he said. Sara followed him.

All three got on the same elevator. Rio by the buttons, Sakuta diagonally behind her, Sara at his side.

"......"

No one said a word.

"Sure is cold today."

"It is."

"Sure is."

"……"

Another silence settled.

In hindsight, this was an awkward grouping. Toranosuke had functionally dumped Sara because he'd fallen for Rio.

The tension remained palpable all the way to the floor the cram school was on.

6

Three answer sheets on the table. From left to right: thirty points, one hundred points, and forty-five points. Kento, Sara, and Juri, respectively.

"Yamada, is thirty your favorite number?"

That had been his score on the midterms, too.

"Sakuta-sensei, don't leak personal info."

Kento tried to hide his grade from Sara, but it was too late. The lack of circles was all too evident. Cross-shaped flowers bloomed everywhere, and Sara had a bird's-eye view.

"Then we'll focus on what Yamada and Yoshiwa got wrong. Himeji, this'll just be review for you."

"Got it."

Worse, the only one *really* listening was Sara, who already understood all this.

Once he'd gone through the explanations, he gave each of them a set of practice problems solved the same way. Three questions total.

Sara had them all done inside ten minutes. She said "Done!" and put her hand up, and her page was covered in neat figures, all answers correct.

He gave her some extra problems and checked on how the other two were doing. Kento was making lots of noises and glaring at one of the problems. Juri's hands had stopped dead on the second problem.

"Yoshiwa, you can solve that with the thing we just covered," he said, pointing at the example still on the whiteboard.

"Like this?" she asked, her hands moving again. Her handwriting was adorable.

"Yeah, and…"

"Sakuta-sensei! Help me out, too!"

"Just a moment, Yamada. Once I'm done with Yoshiwa."

"Uh, I can wait," Juri offered with a brief glance at Kento.

"We're almost done. Go ahead and solve it," Sakuta said, pretending not to notice.

"Yamada, can I help?" Sara asked. She leaned in to look at his page.

"Nah…," Kento said, pulling back.

"Wow, rude," Sara said with a smile.

"I didn't mean it that way!"

"Then let me help."

Sara pulled her chair closer and started going, "Use this formula, like…" while writing directly on his page.

Kento's shoulder was pressing right up against hers, and he'd stopped moving at all. Only his eyes followed what Sara wrote. He was desperately trying to keep it together.

And Juri's pencil stopped again, right before Sakuta's eyes. Her eyes never left the problem. They were pointedly fixed right on her page, but her mind was clearly elsewhere. Entirely focused on what was going on between Sara and Kento.

"Get it?" Sara asked, ducking low to get a better look at his face.

"Y-yeah," he stammered.

"Then give it a try, Yamada."

"Um…I use this formula…"

Kento solved the problem just like she'd taught him to. This mainly consisted of plugging numbers into the formula she'd written out for him. Naturally, that made it easy to get the answer.

"Like that?"

"See, you can do it, Yamada. Try the next one."

"It looks hard."

"Well, with this one…"

Sara was running her pencil across his page again.

"Oh, okay. Then here…?"

Solving one seemed to have given him confidence, and this time he even asked Sara a question of his own.

While Kento made steady progress, Juri's pen was still stuck on the second problem. It didn't seem likely to move anytime soon.

"Uh, Yoshiwa?"

"I get it. I can solve this. I know how."

"If you're sure…"

The class went on, and there were signs of improvement in math—but their relationships seemed to be getting more and more complicated. Sakuta couldn't help much on that front.

"That's all for today," he said as they hit the eighty-minute mark.

"Thanks, Sakuta-sensei!" Kento said, bounding to his feet and shouldering his backpack.

"Make sure to review what you learned today, Yamada."

Kento turned back, one foot out the door, and made a face.

"See you next week at school!" Sara said with a wave. That brightened him up. If he'd had a tail, he'd have wagged it.

"You aren't leaving, Himeji?"

"I've got another class and need Teach's advice."

Sara glanced at Sakuta.

"Ah…"

Wanting to talk to her longer, he tried to come up with another topic but couldn't think of any.

"You're in the way," Juri complained while trying to push past Kento.

"I'm leaving, too!" he said, giving up and moving on.

Sara watched them go, stifling a smirk.

"You shouldn't tease your classmates," Sakuta said as he erased the whiteboard.

"You mean Yamada?" Sara asked. She approached the board to help.

"And Yoshiwa."

That name made her hand stop just above a cosine.

Sakuta erased it for her.

"You're very hands-on with your students, Teach."

"If their grades don't improve, I'm in trouble."

Sara erased the final tangent. Now the whiteboard lived up to its name.

"Okay, I'll stop trying to mess up your classes."

She accepted his criticism easily, seemingly meaning it. But she didn't sound guilty. And her promise was a tacit admission that she'd been doing that deliberately.

He was starting to get why Toranosuke had been concerned.

"But there's nothing I can do about Yamada's feelings."

"That's fine. He'll have to sort those out himself."

"Nothing I can do about Yoshiwa's feelings, either."

"That's fine. She'll have to sort those out herself."

"You're very hands-off with your students, Teach."

This was the exact opposite of her earlier appraisal, delivered with a grin.

He straightened up the whiteboard pens he'd used, and Sara grabbed a stray blue one for him.

"That aside, Teach…"

"Mm?" He accepted the blue pen from her.

"Did you do my homework?"

From the next booth, he could hear a teacher discussing world history. Both found their eyes turning that way.

"Best we talk outside. I'm hungry anyway."

There was no telling who might overhear.

"Oh, I was hoping to grab the new donut from the café by the station."

"I'm not buying."

"Teach, look close."

Sara held up her perfect answer sheet.

"I worked very hard."

She tapped the part that said *100 points* with a triumphant smile.

He made Sara wait twenty minutes while he wrote up his classroom logs, and then they left the cram school together.

The sun had set, but the area around Fujisawa Station was lit up with holiday lights and felt brighter than it did by day.

The temperature had dropped like a stone, and as they walked toward the station, their breaths were white.

"You got plans for Christmas, Teach?"

"If that dream comes true, I'll end up on a date with you."

"A teacher with a student? Scandalous!"

She was clearly joking.

"But why *were* we together?"

"Good question."

He'd yet to uncover any clues.

"Any ideas, Himeji?"

"I've gotta assume you're just cheating, Teach."

"Reeeeal convincing."

"Dripping with sarcasm!"

Laughing, they headed up the stairs to the pedestrian overpass. The café she'd mentioned was just outside the north gates, on the second story of the building opposite the electronics store.

Inside those big glass panes were students studying and suits with their laptops out. Half the seats were occupied. By day, you often couldn't get a seat at all, but at this hour, the crowds had thinned.

It was perfect for their talk.

As they stepped in, the staff greeted them cheerily.

"Find us a seat," Sakuta said, and he moved to the register, where he ordered a hot caffe latte, a caramel latte, and the new Christmas donut. He paid with his IC card and moved his tray to the next counter over.

He glanced at the tables and didn't see Sara anywhere. Her coat and bag were sitting on a table by the windows. He found the girl herself standing by a table closer at hand.

A boy and a girl sat there, wearing Minegahara uniforms. Sara was smiling, and on the surface, they all seemed happy to chat. But behind their smiles, he caught a whiff of unease, possibly desperation. Like both the boy and the girl were forcing their smiles. Was that all in his mind?

Sakuta sat down first, and when Sara spotted him, she bounced back over. She used both hands to pull her chair out and plopped herself down directly across from him. Her eyes locked on the powdered top of the donut.

"Thanks!"

"Don't tell Yamada."

If he heard, he'd try to get free food out of Sakuta, too.

"I'll tell him you'll buy him something if he scores one hundred points."

Sakuta wouldn't have minded if that actually motivated Kento to do better, but he was fairly certain it would just make Kento drop the idea.

"But I bet Yamada would just go, 'Never mind, then.'"

Sara was clearly on the same page as Sakuta.

Laughing, she reached for her pocket and pulled out her phone. She then started taking pictures of her donut and caramel latte. "So cute!" *Snap, snap, snap.*

"You know them?" Sakuta asked, eyes wandering back toward the Minegahara couple.

"She's a friend from class…," Sara said, glancing at the girl. "And the boy she's with is a second-year. I worked with him when we planned the sports festival."

She turned to the boy seated closer to them.

They saw her looking, and she gave them a little wave. They waved back, and then the boy picked up their trays. It was plain to see they were getting ready to leave.

Once they'd deposited their dishes, the girl waved at Sara once more on her way out. They kept waving to each other until the couple was out of sight.

The boy looked rather at a loss the whole time. Sakuta was increasingly sure of it. He seemed very ready to get out of here. Part of that might have just been feeling left out when the two girls started chatting, but there was likely more to it.

"Something between you and the boy?" he asked, sipping at his caffe latte.

"You're a sharp one, Teach," Sara said.

She'd cut her donut into bite-size pieces and popped one into her mouth. "Oh, that's good!" she said with apparent delight. "He asked me out two months back," she added.

"What did you say?"

He could guess the answer. It certainly hadn't been a yes.

"I turned him down. Said I couldn't date him right now."

"Right now."

"Well, it was true! I didn't really know him yet."

"And you told him that?"

"Yep."

That was why he'd looked so uncomfortable. That phrasing made it sound like he still had a shot. Made him pin his hopes on the future.

"Does your friend know he asked you out?"

"I didn't tell her myself, but I bet she knew. Girls can sense these things."

And she'd gone up to talk to them anyway. Talk about moxie.

"Oh, but I don't think they're actually a couple yet. That's why I said to let me know when they are. Personally, I would *never* date someone a friend rejected."

"You could have just let them be."

"Two months is not nearly long enough."

That's how she justified her behavior.

"If he's got no shot at turning your head, I think it's better for him to move on."

"Would it be that easy for him to give up, though? Right after he asked me out?"

She acted like she couldn't believe it.

"I tend to carry a torch myself," Sakuta admitted.

"Teach, sometimes you look like you're lying, and then you say the truth."

"Then are you still in love with Kasai?"

His abrupt swerve made her eyes go wide. She blinked twice. And in that brief moment, she worked out how he knew.

"Aha. Tora-chan...I mean, Kasai-senpai fed you some facts?"

Her deduction was spot on, but she looked a little put out. Sakuta was a little taken aback himself.

"He said you're old friends. And that he was worried about you."

"So he feels guilty about effectively dumping me?" she asked, smiling the whole time.

"More or less."

"I'm more worried about him, frankly. Falling for a prickly customer like Futaba-sensei? She'll never say yes."

"Kasai seems like he'd do well otherwise."

His earnestness came on strong, but fundamentally, he was a good-natured jock.

"He comes across as a good dude."

Sakuta really had only a surface impression at this stage. But Yuuma had also called Toranosuke a "good guy." Since Toranosuke had come to Sakuta at Yuuma's word, Sakuta figured he should take Yuuma at his word, too. Yuuma himself was a good dude, so he should know how to recognize one.

"He is that," Sara said, feigning a pout. "I mean, he's even worried about the girl he dumped."

She couldn't quite bring herself to admit it without a bit of snark. He *had* more or less dumped her, so he likely deserved a little spite.

The way she joked about it now suggested she wasn't still dragging him around. So he felt like he didn't have to make her spell out how she felt right now. He knew.

"When I first learned Kasai-senpai didn't love me, I hated him so much."

Her grimace hid any hint of awkwardness.

"You might already know, but through junior high, everyone thought the two of us were dating."

"So I've heard."

"There were plenty of girls who liked him, but I was the only one allowed to be at his side. I was kinda proud of that, I guess? At least, I didn't object. But when I got to high school..."

"Kasai had fallen for someone else."

Toranosuke had said that, for the first time, he knew what love was.

"That really shook me. I'd thought he was in love with me, and everyone else had said we were good together. But none of that was real. I didn't know what to believe. Couldn't even trust my own mind, much less what anyone else said. I felt like the world as I knew it had been a complete fabrication. And that's when I got really scared. Like everyone had just been laughing at me the whole time. I didn't even want to leave the house."

"This was during Golden Week?"

"Yeah."

"But getting Adolescence Syndrome helped you recover."

She'd said as much before.

"It did."

"I hear you're pretty popular these days. Is that related?"

"Teach, you really did do your homework."

"I'm surprisingly hands-on with my students."

"But wrong answer. Popularity is *not* my Adolescence Syndrome. Honestly, even I'm starting to be like, 'Damn, I've really got it going on.'"

"Seems like you're enjoying it."

He didn't need her to confirm that. Sara's expression was full of life.

"If I admit that, I'll sound like an awful person."

"I think you've got a great personality."

"That doesn't sound like a compliment."

She was clearly enjoying their banter, too. One fun thing made everything else in life a good time. Sara was evidently in the midst of one of those positivity chain reactions.

"You've made it clear, Teach. You don't like me being popular."

"I wouldn't say that. Just…no matter how many people ask you out, no matter how many people hit on you, no matter how much attention you get—that won't get you what you're *really* looking for."

"……What does *that* mean?"

She'd been with him every step of the way, but he'd lost her at last.

"I'm super happy right now. There's nothing missing!"

Sara looked Sakuta right in the eye, demanding a response.

This whole time, she hadn't once said the most important thing. She'd talked about how Toranosuke felt, what their friends had said—but never once spelled out her own feelings. She'd almost answered his first question—but not quite.

Was she still in love with Toranosuke?

Sara had neither confirmed nor denied.

"I just think true happiness doesn't lie in the number of conquests."

"So how do you define it?"

"Okay, let me try…"

Sakuta paused, thinking about Mai.

Someone whose company he enjoyed.

Someone whose laugh was infectious.

Someone he wanted to share his life with.

Mai was all those things.

He channeled those thoughts into a quiet reply.

"In my mind, true happiness comes when the person I love the most loves me the most."

A lot had happened to bring him to that truth. To make those words possible. There was no varnish or veils here. No awkwardness or shame. Just the plain facts.

"If you've got that, you don't need anything else."

"……"

Sara was staring at him so hard she forgot to blink. Her smile had disappeared. It was as if she'd never heard anything like this and didn't know how to respond.

"Let me ask again, Himeji. Do you still love Kasai?"

"……"

Sara didn't answer. Or more likely, *couldn't.*

He'd expected as much. Something had felt off the whole time, since she first joked about his dumping her.

That day, and today, she'd never said a word.

Not about grief.

Not about suffering.

Not about how much she'd cried.

Nothing like that at all.

She'd been upset, yes, but that was because Toranosuke's feelings turned out to be different from what she'd expected. Everyone else's assumption had been wrong. The truth had betrayed her expectations.

"Or even before that—did you ever love him?"

"You're implying I'm just like him?"

"I think it's a distinct possibility."

Everyone had said they were good together, so they'd believed it.

"......Then tell me this," Sara said after a brief pause.

She looked up at him, a challenge in her eyes. And voice.

"How can I love someone the way you do?"

For the first time, Sara managed a genuine answer to his question.

Chapter
3
I need you

1

"Hmm. So now you're giving her firsthand instruction in romance?" Mai said, stabbing a fork into her salad with an audible crunch.

"That's what she asked for, but I offered no guarantees. Not doing firsthand anything."

The weekend was over, and it was Monday, December 12.

The lunch rush was over. Seats were starting to open up in the cafeteria, and the din was starting to die down. The seats on either side of them were empty, too. Which meant they were free to talk about *this*.

"Sakuta, you're trying to figure out this girl's Adolescence Syndrome for me, right?" Mai asked, looking quite bored with her salad.

"Yes. Because you're in danger."

"I fail to see the connection."

The fork left her mouth. Was she intentionally aiming the silver tines at him? Even the most generous read suggested she was.

"Yikes, now you're the danger."

Rio's warning was no laughing matter. This had to be taken care of promptly. But he wasn't sure how to convince Mai.

A well-timed voice saved him from his predicament.

"Mind if I join you?" Miori spotted them and came over.

"Sit anywhere you like, please."

"Oh? Really?" She was the one who asked, so why was she surprised? "You usually say, 'I'd rather you didn't.'"

"I'm in a better mood today," he lied, glancing at the chair.

"Then I'll take you up on that," Miori said. She glanced at him, then at Mai, and sat next to Sakuta.

"......"

"I'd much rather stare at Mai," she explained, answering his unspoken question. "You seemed like you were having fun. What's the topic?"

Miori took a big bite of her *katsu* curry. Her eyes quickly focused on the gleaming fork in Mai's hand. It was very Miori to pick up on the tension between them and characterize it as "fun."

"We're talking about how to fall in love."

"Deep."

She sounded impressed.

"Oh? It's pretty basic," he said. That was the opposite take.

"But what brought this on?"

"This cutie Sakuta teaches asked about it."

"A girl, then?"

Was it necessary to clarify that?

"A female student, yes."

"Yikes."

Miori made a show of disgust. Like he was a dirty old teacher. But the joke soon faded.

"Still, I guess I get that," she continued. "I've wondered what love is myself."

A bite of *katsu* vanished between her lips. Sitting next to her, Sakuta could hear her chewing.

"You a *katsu* curry fan, Mitou?"

"Love it."

She took another big spoonful.

"Then that's what love is."

But Sakuta's courteous explanation provoked a scowl. He could tell from her eyes that she already had a complaint ready, but her mouth was too full to actually talk yet.

She chewed for a minute, then swallowed. She chased that with a big gulp of water. When she finally did speak, she was looking at Mai instead.

"Mai, what made you fall for Azusagawa?"

"Excellent question, Mitou," he said, following her gaze.

Miori was likely hoping Mai would help her get back at him. It was obvious she was expecting Mai to unleash a tongue-lashing. But this was a doomed strategy. Whether Mai chose to actually answer the question or scold him, Sakuta would deem it a reward.

Both sets of eyes were on Mai.

"He loves me."

"……"

Miori's hand paused halfway to her mouth. She clearly hadn't expected that good of an answer. Her spoon wavered in midair.

"An adage to live by," she whispered at last. Her spoon dived back into the curry as she forgot her original purpose in favor of savoring Mai's words. "Oh. Yeah. That would do it," she muttered.

"Not gonna ask me why I love Mai?"

"I know that already."

At this point, Mai's phone vibrated. She snatched it off the table and answered it.

"Yes, no problem. Okay, on my way."

She hung up and tucked it in her purse.

"Ryouko's here to pick me up, so I've gotta run."

"Headed to work, Mai?" Miori asked.

Sakuta had prior warning. She was filming a commercial for a moisturizer that made your skin glow. A perfect fit for Mai.

"Yep. Later!" Mai flashed a smile and got to her feet.

"I'll clear your dishes."

"Thanks. Please."

Mai shouldered her purse, waved the hand with her ring, and left the cafeteria.

*   *   *

Once Mai was off to work, Sakuta relaxed in the emptying cafeteria long enough to enjoy a cup of tea. As he did, he told Miori just a bit about his student—Sara. Of course, he left out the Adolescence Syndrome.

By the time he had more or less explained the situation, it was time for him to head to third-period class. From the cafeteria, it was about a hundred yards to the main class building.

"That girl's something else."

"Mm?"

"Your student."

"The way the boys all fall for her?"

"More the way she's enjoying being the envy of every other girl."

"You're not enjoying that?"

From what he could see, Miori was just as popular. Simply walking with her like this, he could see boys looking. And the other girls picked up on that, which made it all too easy to court jealousy.

In actual fact, at the party for their shared core class, she'd found herself targeted by a dude her friend had been hoping to land. He'd gone so far as to try to get her number. She'd wound up at Sakuta's table trying to extract herself from trouble.

That had likely caused some lingering resentment. For all he knew, her friend was still not over it.

"I can't, no. They're mad at me but feel like they can't win—so they just give up. But there's advantages to having me around, so they can't quite bring themselves to cut me loose—and that makes me go, 'What a pain.'"

She kept her tone light, but she was being pretty brutal. He was genuinely impressed Miori could say all this without rancor. It convinced him that she wasn't holding a grudge or anything.

"I mean, it's not like I don't get any smug sense of superiority out of it."

She neatly wrapped things up like it was all a laughing matter.

"Superiority, hmm?"

That wasn't necessarily a bad thing. It was an emotion that went hand in hand with confidence.

"With Himeji, I think that's winning out over all other emotions."

"She must like herself a lot, then. Far more than she does anyone else."

"……"

To Miori, that might well have just been an off-the-cuff observation. It sounded like one. But to Sakuta, those uncannily accurate words lifted the fog lingering in his mind in the blink of an eye.

It seemed like Miori had managed to encapsulate Sara with a simple comment.

He remembered Tomoe's take.

Sara had been sought-after even in junior high, and Tomoe wasn't exactly comfortable around her. Her feelings sprang from lingering inadequacy—Tomoe had remade herself at the start of high school. Part of her felt like a fraud and thought Sara was the real deal.

Sara's cheer was free of spite.

She was friendly without malice.

Even when she'd been teasing Kento, it didn't come from a bad place. She didn't let it feel that way. And that's why he hadn't taken it badly.

Sara was accustomed to being liked.

It came naturally to her.

Using the right words and gestures were a part of her.

None of it was forced.

She didn't have to work for it.

There had never been a reason to question why she was always at the center of the crowd—that's what had taught her to act this way.

From what Toranosuke had told him, Sara had been in an enviable position in junior high, elementary school, even kindergarten.

That was how her life had always been; it was normal to her. Everyone looked at her different—and she took that for granted. She'd been standing at the center of the crowd for so long she never questioned it.

But because her classroom life had been so fulfilling, because she'd been so socially blessed—perhaps she'd fallen into a huge trap without even realizing it.

Affection was something others gave her.

All she'd ever done was accept it.

Jealousy was an inevitable side effect. To her mind, it might even be a spice that constantly boosted her confidence.

And after so much time spent like that, rather than love another—she'd learned to love being loved.

Miori's words had suggested as much.

"If you want insight into a popular girl, ask another."

"I'm full of insights," Miori boasted.

"Then let me also ask—what do you think I should *do*?"

"About your adorable student?"

She put a teasing lilt on *adorable*.

"Yeah, the cutie."

Sakuta wasn't one to let that get to him. Sara's cuteness level was an objective fact.

"Do what she says and teach her how to love like you do."

"How?"

"Make her fall in love with you."

Miori didn't even get the whole line out before she broke up laughing.

"Brilliant idea," Sakuta said, looking revolted. That was clearly the response she'd wanted.

As proof, her grin broadened. "I swear I won't tell Mai," she insisted.

"Gee, thanks."

"Oh, but you'd best be careful, Azusagawa," she said, giving him some side-eye.

"Careful of what?"

"Isn't it obvious? You're walking into the spider's lair. Don't become her *third* horndog teacher."

She was laughing at her own joke before she even finished it.

"I belong to Mai."

"Reeeeally? I haven't heard you talk about anyone but this cutie-patootie student today."

"……"

That cut him to the quick.

"And isn't that exactly what your student *wants*, Azusagawa-sensei?"

She really did know where to stick that knife.

Maybe Sara already had her threads wound around him. If he wasn't careful, he might well end up trapped in her web. Just imagining that made him grimace.

"I'll be careful."

Listening to Miori's flawless advice had brought them to the classroom building. It was almost time for third period to begin.

2

Two days later. Wednesday, December 14. Sakuta had class through fourth period, turned down Takumi's invite to a mixer, and went straight to Fujisawa Station.

But once there, he headed not to his apartment, but the other way— toward the cram school.

He reached it just after five thirty. He put his things away and changed, then moved to the teacher's room and prepped for class.

He prepared some problems so Kento and Juri could review what they'd learned last time.

For Sara, he found a few problems that were more college-entrance-exam level. He tried to match the difficulty of what could be expected on the Common Test. He was adding a few geared more toward top universities when he felt someone staring at him.

He looked up and found Juri watching him over the counter between the teachers' area and the free space.

"Um, Azusagawa-sensei," she said when their eyes met. She'd been reluctant to interrupt his work.

"What's up, Yoshiwa?"

It wasn't often she came to him. He got up and came over to the counter.

"Is it possible to shift the date of next Saturday's class?"

"Sure, but…?"

Did she have other plans?

"I've got a beach volleyball tournament. Forgot to mention it earlier, sorry."

"You play this time of year?"

To Sakuta, the sport was synonymous with midsummer sun. White sand. Tanned skin and colorful swimsuits.

"It was supposed to be in September but got postponed because of a typhoon."

"All the way to December?"

"It's in Okinawa."

"I guess it's still warm enough down there."

The photo Shouko had included in a recent letter had suggested everyone was still dressed for summer.

"This late in the year, most of us will be wearing something warmer."

"You've got options there?"

Lots of new info here. He'd assumed you could only play in summer.

"Either way, fine by me. Good luck in the tournament."

"Okay. Thank you."

"When do you want the lesson?" he asked, looking at the calendar.

"Are you open on the twenty-third?"

"Sure. That'll work."

"Good."

They'd said what needed to be said, and the conversation petered out.

"......"

Juri wasn't saying anything, but she was decidedly also not going away.

"Anything else?" he prompted. Her shoulders twitched.

"......Um, this is about a friend," Juri said, her voice very soft, her eyes studying the pattern on the countertop. She didn't intend to do that and possibly didn't even realize she was. Her mind was entirely on things unconnected to her vision.

"Uh-huh, a friend."

"I had a dream where they asked someone out and got rejected."

"That #dreaming thing's really going around."

"Yeah. And...what do you think I should do?"

"We talking about Yamada and Himeji?"

"?!"

She neither confirmed nor denied. It was simply complete and utter surprise. Too shocked to say a word. Her face silently screamed "How?!"

"I mean, Yamada's pretty obvious."

"......"

Again, Juri hadn't said yes or no. She just seemed perplexed, maybe a bit mad. Or perhaps she was just trying to calm herself down.

"But doesn't that work in your favor?"

"......Absolutely not. I don't want that awful girl toying with the boy I like."

Her eyes shook more than her voice did. Both were filled with frustration and anger.

"If it's getting under your skin that bad, you better make him yours."

"I can't," Juri snapped.

Instant refusal, not even enough of a gap for light to seep in.

"How can I compete with Himeji?" she croaked, so quiet he barely caught it. Her gaze was on the counter again. No, even lower than that. Now it was all the way down at her feet.

He knew Sara was a hit with the boys.

But he didn't think Juri was lagging as far behind as she thought. At the very least, there was no reason for her to be this pessimistic.

"Don't be mad at me for suggesting this…"

"……What?"

Her eyes rose a bit, but she already sounded grumpy. It probably wasn't that she was mad at Sakuta. Just that this unpleasant subject was putting her in a bad mood.

But when Juri's eyes met his, he caught a hint of expectation. She had wound up latching onto the countertop, eagerly waiting for his next words.

"With Yamada, flash him your tan lines, and you'll kill him dead."

"……"

She didn't respond right away.

Perhaps she hadn't quite processed what he'd said. Her face never moved. She blinked several times.

At long last, realization dawned, and her gaze shifted right and left.

"……Really?"

He'd half expected her to lash out, but instead he got a very faint request for confirmation. She wasn't quite looking at him. But the light of hope was definitely brighter.

Maybe this was the wrong advice to give.

"I certainly think so."

But he couldn't back off now. He'd meant it, so it was best to stick to his guns.

"……"

Juri went real quiet again. Thinking. Sakuta would have loved to know what she made of his suggestion, but time did not allow for that.

"'Sup!" came the cheery (yet also unmotivated) voice of the subject at hand. Kento. "Oh, Sakuta-sensei, how's it hanging?"

Juri didn't turn to look. She kept her back to him, so he couldn't see her face—which had gone bright red.

"Well, if everyone's here, let's start class."

"Mm? Is Himeji already here?" Kento asked, obliviously putting that name out there.

No wonder Juri's hands tightened on the strap of her bag.

"Himeji's getting a different lesson, so I told her come in later."

"H-huh…," Kento said, shoving his hands in his pockets. Feigning indifference.

"I'll be right there, so wait inside."

"Sakuta-sensei, what's on the curriculum?"

"Review of last time."

"I never wanna see another sine or cosine!"

"We've got tangents, too."

"You're killing me!" Kento wailed, and he trailed off into the cubicle. Juri glared at his back the whole time.

Class began at six and lasted eighty minutes, wrapping up on time at 7:40.

"Good work, Yamada. That's all for today."

"Finally! This place's classes are waaaaay too long."

They were certainly much longer than high school classes. Likely felt twice as long.

"At college, you'll get some ninety-minute lectures."

"I'm definitely not going to college. I've made up my mind, right here and now."

Kento flopped onto the table.

"Oh, right, Yamada."

"What?"

Kento turned his head so he could see.

"About next Saturday. Mind if we move it to the twenty-third?"

"Mm? Legit? I get next Saturday off?"

"Postponed."

The actual number of classes was unchanged. But Kento was entirely fixated on the upcoming day off.

"But why?"

"Yoshiwa's got a match in Okinawa."

"Oh, the nationals?"

Juri had been putting her pencils away, but Kento swung around to talk to her.

"Yeah."

"As a first-year? That's wild!"

"It's nothing special."

"It totally is. Good luck!"

"……"

She hadn't expected that, and she froze for a second, expressionless. Then she let her guard down.

"Thank you," she said and immediately regretted it, her gaze swimming. Her eyes were practically spinning. Fortunately, Kento was flat out on the desk and couldn't see this. "Bye," Juri said, and she left the room alone, not even putting her coat on, just carrying it with her bag. She was literally fleeing.

That left just Sakuta and Kento. He stayed sprawled out on the table, not budging.

"You aren't leaving, Yamada?"

He was usually the first out the door. Like he couldn't bear to spend a second longer than he had to here. But not today.

"Uh, Sensei…"

"What?"

"Is Himeji seeing anyone?"

"You're her classmate. You know more than I do."

"Well, it doesn't seem like she is."

"But?"

"Does she have her heart set on someone?"

"Sounds like a question for her, not me."

"I'm asking you 'cause I can't ask her! Will you ask for me?"

"Hell no."

"Please!"

Head still down, Kento clasped his hands together.

And someone sneaked into the room behind him.

"Oh, was class still in session?"

It was the topic du jour, Sara.

She looked at Kento the petitioner and Sakuta the patron.

"This doesn't look like class," she said with a giggle.

"Yamada has a question for you."

"Hey! Sakuta-sensei!"

Kento bolted upright. He moved so fast he practically flew to his feet.

"What is it, Yamada?"

"N-nothing important."

"Then just ask. I'm dying to know!"

She turned his own words against him, leaving him nowhere to run.

"Uh, so...I mean, it's almost Christmas."

"Mm-hmm."

Kento had started miles from the field. Did he have a plan to actually reach the goalposts? Didn't seem likely.

"And there's tons of new couples at school."

"Makes you feel left out, huh?"

"Himeji, are you seeing anyone now? Sakuta-sensei and I were wondering."

A hard left toward the goal line...then he abruptly roped Sakuta in. Sara had been staring fixedly at him the whole time, which explained why he swerved at the last second.

Sakuta wasn't thrilled that he had been dragged in, but he could tell this had been a solid effort on Kento's part.

But he'd made one fatal error. Sara had a powerful counter ready.

"Why would *you* want to know?"

"Huh? Why…?"

Kento had given up on facing her. His feeble gaze was locked on Sakuta now, pleading for a rescue.

Fine, just this once, Sakuta thought.

"If you're taken, we can't exactly have classes over Christmas."

"Pretty sure you're the one who doesn't wanna schedule anything then, Teach."

His plan was simple—make himself the target.

"Yep, vehemently against it."

"Sensei, which matters more? Us, or your girlfriend?"

"Please. My girlfriend."

"You don't have to be so blunt about it! Why are you getting all serious on us?" Sara asked, feigning anger but smiling.

"Exactly, Sensei."

Making him the bad guy helped Kento make a clean getaway. He was also putting his coat on and getting ready to go. He owed Sakuta big-time for this.

"Then I'm outta here!" he said, and he turned to go.

"Oh, Yamada," Sara said.

"Mm? What?"

She'd said his name, so he had to turn back. The tension in his body was almost palpable.

"I'm not dating anyone, but I do have my eye on someone."

"……"

Kento's jaw dropped. He started to say something, but his mouth just opened and closed, only gurgling noises coming out. No human speech.

"That's all! Bye!"

Sara gave him a wave, and Kento returned it on pure reflex. He managed a grunt that sort of sounded like it meant something, then drifted away like a dead man walking.

Leaving just Sara and Sakuta behind.

She took a seat as if nothing had happened. Pulled her pen case and notes from her backpack, then looked up to meet his gaze.

"This is your fault for bringing up the subject, Teach."

"I'm not criticizing."

"But you are going, 'She did it again!'"

"I'm impressed. It was undeniably impressive."

"But you mean that sarcastically."

"I mean it in all sorts of ways."

"Then what should I have done? We're in class. Teach me."

"Okay, solve these first."

Sakuta slapped two worksheets on the table.

"First page is at the difficulty of the Common Test. Second is taken from past tests at a notoriously tough school. They're all quadratic equation."

"And solving these will help me fall in love like you, Teach?"

"They'll give me an idea of your current academic level. You've got forty minutes."

He showed Sara the timer and clicked start.

She seemed like she wasn't done talking, but when she heard the beep, she resigned herself and started working her way through the problems. That was definitely her straight-A student side. The only outward sign of her silent protest was her pursed lips.

While he waited, Sakuta took a look at the same problems. If he couldn't solve them, he could hardly explain them to her.

First, the Common Test sheet. He managed all three problems without issue.

Next, the old exam questions for the tough college. These were not as easy. When he'd picked them out, he'd seen the model answers and thought he understood, but when he actually tried to come up with a solution on his own, he discovered he didn't really get it.

That would hardly do, so Sakuta grabbed a study guide. While he was wrestling with the explanations there, time passed—and forty minutes ran out before he'd finished solving it. The timer chirped, and they were done.

Sara let out a little sigh and put her pencil down. Hands on the desk, like she'd just finished a test. She did not look pleased.

"Well?"

"I could only solve the first two."

There had been five total. Three for the Common Test and two from the tough college.

"That's plenty good at your stage."

She was still a first-year. It would be two more years before she'd need to sit the real exam.

He checked her work in the notebook. The two she'd deemed "solved" did indeed show the right answers.

The third problem was one of those trick questions. Sara had fallen for the trap and tried to solve it the wrong way. It looked like she'd figured out something was wrong halfway but didn't have enough time to figure out the real answer.

"Then let's start with problem three."

He wrote the model answer on the whiteboard. As he scrawled the first formula on the board, Sara went, "Oh, you use *that* one?!"

She'd already realized her mistake.

"Yeah, the function here is unrelated."

As long as you made the right initial choice, the rest of the calculations were pretty simple. The problem tested your language skills more than your knowledge of math.

The trick was a good one, cleverly disguised as a different type of problem, and Sara's attempted solution had used the wrong method.

Students who'd mastered those strategies were all the more likely to succumb to this quagmire.

"Teach, this problem is just like you."

"I'm not nearly this devious."

"I do love that brazen streak."

"Next problem."

"Don't just blow off your student's confessions!"

"I don't mind that side of you, Himeji."

"……"

Sara's eyes went wide in apparent surprise.

Paying that no heed, he turned around and drew a quadratic function graph on the board.

"But it concerns me if you act that way around anyone else."

"……What does that mean?"

"Exactly, that's the whole problem. This simple y = x messes everything up."

"That's not what I'm asking about! Explain yourself, Teach!"

Sakuta stopped writing and turned to look at her.

"……"

She was staring up at him.

How should he phrase this?

As she watched him search for the right words, a smile played across her lips.

And behind her—Rio walked past the entrance to the classroom.

"Oh, Futaba! Wait up!"

Rio stopped and came back.

"What?"

"C'mere a sec."

He beckoned, and she frowned but stepped in.

"Aren't you teaching?" she asked, glancing at Sara.

"I don't really get this problem. Bail me out!"

"Some cram school teacher you are."

"Please!"

He handed the problem over, and Rio ran her eyes over it. She considered it for maybe thirty seconds, then erased everything he'd written on the whiteboard.

Then she redrew the entire graph, explaining what the graph meant and how it represented the function. She didn't neglect any of the necessary calculations, either.

This was a problem so hard Sakuta had been baffled by it for a solid twenty minutes, and Rio had it handled inside five.

When she was done, the whiteboard was completely covered.

"Did you get that?" Rio asked, popping the cap on the marker.

"Completely," Sakuta said before Sara could answer.

He'd taken a seat next to her and was listening with rapt attention.

"I wasn't asking you, Azusagawa." Her voice curt.

Rio's eyes were on Sara, who nodded.

"I followed you just fine," she admitted. "It was very clear."

"Math isn't your only good subject, right?" Sakuta asked.

Sara and Rio both looked at him. Half confusion, but the other half was likely suspicion.

"They're definitely not bad, but...," Sara said, clearly not following.

"Average grades in first term?"

"Somewhere between an eight and a nine."

That was even better than he'd imagined. There was a good chance that was her grade for most classes, with the odd seven or ten mixed in. Hard for him to imagine, personally, but Mai's report cards had been pretty much exactly the same.

"Himeji, if you get a proper teacher instructing you, you'll likely pass the toughest college exams on the first try."

Rio saw where he was going with this and shot him a mildly annoyed look.

"What's that supposed to mean?"

"Even you thought Futaba was better at this than I am."

The harder the problem, the more that trend was evident.

"Having her teach you…"

Before he could finish, Sara blurted, "I've *got* a teacher." There was a real urgency in her tone.

"……"

She hadn't raised her voice. But there was a flat rejection there that cut off all further argument. The air in the room turned to ice. Brittle, like it would shatter at a touch. And as the moment lingered, a chilly tension spread.

Rio looked taken aback. Sakuta hid it but was surprised himself. This was the first time Sara had really let her emotions show.

But Sara herself seemed more shocked than anyone.

That she'd spoken on impulse.

That she'd let her emotions control her.

That she'd spoken louder than she meant to—all of that seemed to come as a surprise to her.

"Something going on in here? Everything okay?"

The principal poked his head in. He'd likely been roaming the classrooms, scoping things out.

He looked at Sara's back first, then gave Sakuta a concerned look. Probably because he knew Sakuta was Sara's third teacher. And knew what had happened to the previous two.

"Sorry. I didn't prep properly for this problem and had to ask Futaba to bail me out," Sakuta explained.

"Yeah?"

Sara nodded at the principal's response, and once she did, Rio confirmed it.

Then they fell silent again.

This was broken by the timer signaling the end of class. The tone of it was disconcertingly jaunty. But it was more than enough of an excuse to get up.

"Thanks for today," Sara said, eyes down. She gathered up her things and grabbed her coat. "See you next time," she added, bowing her head. With that, she left the class.

The principal almost said something but ultimately decided against it. Instead, he turned to Sakuta.

"Everything okay?" he asked again, not being at all specific. It wasn't hard to tell that he didn't want to go into specifics.

So Sakuta kept it vague, just saying, "Yeah." It meant nothing. Merely a ritual to allow them all to go their separate ways.

"Well, good luck," he said and left the room.

His footsteps faded away.

That left Sakuta and Rio here with this mood.

Rio took a deep breath, then asked, "What was that for?" Her tone was unmistakably interrogative.

"What do you mean?"

"You intentionally pissed her off, right?"

She phrased it as a question but was clearly harboring no doubts.

Since he'd roped her in, he owed her that much explanation.

"Long story short, I'm protecting Mai."

That was pretty much the only thing on his mind, these days.

"So it's all connected to those messages somehow? The ones telling you Sakurajima was in danger and to find Touko Kirishima?" Rio asked.

He nodded.

"Futaba, we talked about whether Touko Kirishima herself means Mai harm or whether someone she gave Adolescence Syndrome to will end up posing a threat."

"And the former isn't likely, right?"

"Yeah."

He'd reached that conclusion after talking to Touko.

"So if we focus on the second idea... Azusagawa, you've worked out what her Adolescence Syndrome is?"

"Not in the slightest."

"……Now I'm confused."

She rarely scrunched her face up to this much.

"I don't know what the symptoms are, but I've got a pretty good hunch on what caused it."

That should be enough for Rio to connect the dots.

"……Oh, I get it. That's just like you, Azusagawa. You're trying to cure her Adolescence Syndrome by solving the problem she has, figuring you don't need to know what her symptoms actually are."

"Good plan, right?"

Every case they'd encountered linked directly to matters of the heart. That was the crux of the issue. If his main goal was to cure her, it didn't actually matter what supernatural stuff was going on with Sara. He just had to fix the real issue. An alternative solution. There was more than one path to the desired outcome.

"But winding up a high school girl like that isn't very mature of you."

"She might hold a grudge."

"You want her to. But…even if that's what you were aiming for, her response was a bit extreme, right?"

"Oh, that's on you."

"Is it?"

"I told you why Himeji got Adolescence Syndrome, right?"

"Someone broke her heart?"

"And that someone was Kasai."

"……"

Rio's jaw literally dropped.

"Azusagawa," she hissed.

"Mm?"

"When you drag me in, tell me the reason *first*."

"If I had, would you have helped?"

"In a case like this, absolutely not."

That's why he hadn't told her. Plus, he didn't actually have a chance to anyway.

3

The next day was a Thursday, and Sakuta woke up to find it already raining.

All those bright, dry winter days meant the rain came as a boon. The temperature itself held steady, yet it felt warmer—the humidity at work, perhaps?

But once the rain stopped, temperatures would drop heading into the weekend. On TV, the weather girl was dressed for the season. "We're in for some real winter chill!" she said.

"Christmas *was* really cold in that dream."

It was too early for thoughts that gloomy. Sakuta left the house with his umbrella open.

Other than the rain, the morning commute was unremarkable. Fujisawa Station, the Tokaido Line interior, and the hubbub as he switched trains at Yokohama Station...all was the same as always.

No different from yesterday, the day before, or one week ago. The same streets, the same crowds.

The only real difference was on the Keikyu Line from Yokohama Station, where there was a notable lack of trains that played music as they pulled out. Encountering one of those had always made his day, and knowing they'd retired the last few from service was a real shame. One less thing to look forward to on the way to school.

It might seem like the world never changed, but it always was, bit by bit.

End-of-term classes were nearly all finished, and the ones that were left mainly focused on outlining the papers required to get credit or reviewing what would be covered in the tests they'd be taking early next year.

His first class was primary foreign language studies—English—and the test would involve written and listening components. Second period was core curriculum and required a paper. Third period was the core math required for his statistical science major, and it was obviously going to be a test. His fourth class involved computer data processing, and the teacher had an out-of-the-box assignment to create a home page.

When that class wrapped up, he heard friends talking all around. "What about this assignment?" "When do we start?" "It's not due till next year! We got time!" Didn't seem like anyone planned to tackle it immediately. Chattering away, the classroom emptied out.

In the hall, he could hear the subject already drifting away. "I'm starving! Let's eat!" "I'm broke!"

Sakuta alone stayed at his desk, searching for #dreaming posts involving Mai Sakurajima.

If anyone had a dream about something bad happening to her, he might learn the truth behind that ominous message.

Mai's fame made this approach possible.

But like his previous attempts, he found no relevant messages online.

He tried searching for Touko Kirishima next.

If he could glean any more intel there, maybe he'd figure out why he was supposed to find her.

But once again, he found nothing that seemed connected.

Just off-base speculation claiming Mai Sakurajima *was* Touko Kirishima.

———**Their singing voices sound alike!**

———**She hummed on that one TV show, you could tell!**

———**I hear they're going public soon!**

All of them were trying to sound legit, but they were just talking out their asses.

Mai was obviously not Touko.

Sakuta knew that for a fact.

But plenty of people seemed to buy into the rumors.

Perhaps Sakuta only felt this way because he knew them both personally. If he weren't that involved, then why doubt the rumors? Maybe he'd have just gone, "Oh yeah?" If people didn't really care if it was true or not, these reactions made sense.

That was how baseless speculation spread like wildfire.

"Whatcha looking at, Azusagawa?"

The voice from the seat next to him was from Takumi, who'd stuck around without a word.

"A headache."

It was hard to explain the whole thing, so he just answered evasively.

"That sounds like one!"

Takumi just laughed, not pursuing it further.

"What about you, Fukuyama?"

Takumi's eyes were on his screen, and he looked unusually absorbed. Sakuta had been wondering why.

"At the school festival, they did that beauty contest, picking a Mr. and Miss Campus?"

"So I heard."

That had been in early November, nearly a month ago now.

Sakuta hadn't checked out the contest himself, but Nodoka and Sweet Bullet had been invited as presenters and had handed the trophies to the winners.

"And this site lists past winners."

"Checking to see which one was cutest?"

A very guy thing to do. He could just picture a group gathering around going, "Oh, I like her." "Nah, man, this one's way better."

"I meant to, but there's no profile listed for last year's girl. Just the mister!"

"The site made a mistake?"

"With the *miss* contest?"

"……"

"Look, that one's on you."

"……"

"The silent treatment?!"

Ignoring him, Sakuta reached for his mouse and went back to the Touko Kirishima search results. But the table quivered; Takumi's phone was resting on it, and the vibrations were making it slide.

He glanced that way, saw the screen, and recognized the name.

Ryouhei Kodani, a second-year international business major they'd met at the mixer.

"Yeah, what up?" Takumi asked, answering.

"Had a dropout on a mixer today. You in, Fukuyama?"

The phone's volume was loud enough that Sakuta could hear every word.

"You know I am!"

Not a second's thought.

"Yeah? Cool, I'll send the deets over."

"Can't wait!"

After that brief exchange, Takumi hung up. He jumped to his feet, put his coat on, and shouldered his backpack.

"I'm outta here!"

He threw up a hand and headed to the door.

"Your computer's still on!" Sakuta said.

"Kill it for me!"

The answer came from the hall.

He'd run off without even hearing who else was in this mixer, so Sakuta said a prayer for his well-being and grabbed the mouse to shut down Takumi's computer.

But his hand stopped there, not moving another millimeter.

His eyes were glued to the screen.

To the female winner of last year's beauty contest.

Takumi had said she had no profile, but it was there, all right.

Takumi just couldn't see it.

He hadn't been able to perceive it.

Long, well-maintained black hair.

Clean white blouse.

A slightly embarrassed smile directed at the camera from a face he knew.

The miniskirt Santa spotted on campus.

Touko Kirishima herself.

He read the rest of the profile.

And didn't recognize the name at the top.

"Nene Iwamizawa?"

In other words, Touko Kirishima was a stage name.

She'd been a sophomore last year, so if she'd finished the year out, she should currently be a junior. If she'd gotten into college on her first try, she was two years older than him.

Her major was international liberal arts, just like Mai and Nodoka.

She hailed from Hokkaido, her birthday was March 30, and she was five foot three

That's all the profile told him.

This chance encounter sure gave him a rush. Like he'd witnessed a spectacle firsthand, it left his heart racing. But the more he thought about it, all he'd learned was her real name, major, school year, place of birth, date of birth, and height.

It was all surface details. Nothing that got to Touko's essence.

But perhaps this would lead him to that.

Hoping as much, he typed "Nene Iwamizawa" into his keyboard and clicked the search button.

4

Sakuta finally shut the computer down a full hour after he'd started searching for Nene Iwamizawa. It was just past six.

He left the building, his echoing footsteps the only thing that made sound. The rain had kept the skies dark all day, but now it actually *was* dark. The lights were on in the tree-lined path, and it already felt like night.

But there were still scattered students around. As Sakuta headed out, a student in a white coat went the other way. Likely a fourth-year working on their research for their thesis. They were carrying a store bag with some instant noodles and a bottle of coffee inside.

Maybe Sakuta would wind up like that one day.

With that in mind, he headed to the station just in time to board an express.

After twenty minutes rocking on the Keikyu Line, he switched trains at Yokohama Station, as did so many others.

Another twenty minutes rocking on the Tokaido Line.

When he reached Fujisawa Station, it was just past seven, and the place was packed with grown-ups.

This rain just wouldn't quit, and he grumbled about that but opened his umbrella and headed home.

His mind on other things, he let his feet carry him down the roads to his apartment.

He'd learned several things while searching.

The first hit for Nene Iwamizawa had been her own social media account. One with photos accompanied by brief captions.

Browsing that proved that even before the beauty contest, she'd been getting modeling work—since her second year of high school, back in Hokkaido.

She'd moved to Kanagawa Prefecture for college.

The beauty contest results had helped her land a modeling agency and gigs with fashion magazines.

The account seemed proud of her gradually increasing work offers. But things only went smoothly until spring of this year. The last update was April 6.

"Maybe that's when people stopped seeing her."

To Sakuta's knowledge, he was the only one who could see Touko as a miniskirt Santa. Nobody else could perceive her at all. She couldn't exactly model like that.

But this social media account never once mentioned Touko Kirishima. He didn't see a word about music anywhere.

Had she simply kept her modeling career separate from it?

Only she knew the reasoning behind that.

"I'll have to ask the next time we meet."

As he reached that conclusion, he found a familiar vehicle parked outside his building.

A white minivan.

The one driven by Ryouko Hanawa, Mai's manager.

He approached and found her in the driver's seat.

She bobbed her head when she saw him coming, and he bowed back.

But her gaze soon shifted away, to the door of his building. He followed that and saw Mai coming out.

When she moved to open her umbrella, Sakuta came over and held his up.

"Welcome back, Sakuta. You're awfully late."

"Good to be home, Mai. I was looking into some things."

"College homework?"

"The other homework."

"Get anywhere?"

"I didn't learn enough to make that claim, so not sure what I should say."

He'd reached no conclusions, so any attempt to explain would be a mess.

"Well, no time now, so I'll call this evening."

"Off to work, Mai?"

"Work's tomorrow; today's just getting there. I'm making an appearance at a film festival in Fukuoka."

"Does this involve a nice dress?"

"It does. A really gorgeous one."

"Wish I could see that."

"Ryouko will be taking lots of pictures."

"I meant in person."

Mai started walking, so he headed toward the van's back seat, too, keeping her dry. The sliding door opened automatically to greet her.

"I made dinner for you and Kaede, so eat that together."

Mai climbed inside and put her seat belt on. And thanked him for the umbrella.

"Oh, Sakuta…"

"Yes?"

"I've got that Hakone hot springs reservation booked."

"For Christmas?"

"If you're available."

"I will be! I swear!"

"If you can't make it, Ryouko says she'll go with me. No need to bend over backward."

"I've always wanted to stay there," Ryouko cut in with a joke—no, she probably did want to stay there. There was a Hakone guidebook on the seat. She was raring to go.

"Well, if that happens, enjoy it for me," he said.

"I'm not looking forward to being with Mai in *that* mood."

"You're both incorrigible."

Sakuta and Ryouko laughed out loud. Still chuckling, he took a step back from the door and nodded to Ryouko.

The door slid shut, locking into place like a jigsaw puzzle.

The van pulled slowly away, fading into the night. For a minute, he could still see the taillights, but then those disappeared around a corner.

5

"A hot springs with Mai. Can't wait!"

Settling into the tub, he found those words bubbling out of him.

The warmth permeated his body. His belly was full of Mai's cabbage rolls in consommé. His heart was full of thoughts of their Christmas getaway.

But he had good reason not to count his chickens.

"Sure would be great if we could clear all this up by Christmas…"

Chances of that happening were dim.

Today was the fifteenth. He had barely over a week.

Could he cure Touko Kirishima's Adolescence Syndrome by then?

Could he cure Sara Himeji's?

The former was nigh hopeless. He'd made some progress today, but he had failed to obtain anything that got to the crux of Touko's issues.

Sara's issues also seemed unlikely to wrap up that soon. He'd have to see how she responded in their next class; it could still go either way.

Ultimately, Adolescence Syndrome lay in the heart of the individual. No matter how much Sakuta poked and prodded, in the long run Sara would have to work things out herself. He couldn't do everything for her. He never had, and that was not about to change.

"What happens, happens."

He gave up worrying about it, and since he was thoroughly warm, he got out of the bath.

In the changing room, he dried his hair with a towel, then dried his body top to bottom. As he did, the phone rang.

"Sakuta! Unknown number!" Kaede called.

"Can you grab it?"

An unknown number might well by Touko. In which case, he couldn't let this chance pass by. He wanted to talk to her every chance he got. Each opportunity got him a little closer to knowing who she was. And that might let him find a thread leading to a cure for her Adolescence Syndrome.

"Eh, I don't wanna…"

But despite her grumbling, the ringing stopped.

Kaede *had* picked up the receiver.

Sakuta hastily finished drying and put his underwear on.

"……Yes, that's right."

As he stepped out into the living room like that, he saw Kaede with the phone to her ear.

"Sakuta, someone from the cram school," she said, holding it out.

"Who…?"

"Some guy."

Clueless, he took the phone.

"Hello? Sakuta here," he said.

"Oh, Azusagawa!"

The principal's voice.

"What's this about?"

"Sorry to call this late. We just got word from Himeji."

"What about?"

Sara's name made him ask again.

"Nothing major. She just wanted to know your number. Something about wanting to discuss the date of your next class, but since the number's personal information, I wanted to check with you first."

"Oh, thanks. I don't mind. Feel free to give her my number."

"Okay. Keep up the good work."

"Will do."

He waited for the click, then put the receiver down.

He figured it would ring in a few minutes, once Sara had the number.

The principal was likely calling her back right now.

How long would it take for her to write the number down, thank him, and hang up?

His phone could ring at any minute.

But five minutes passed, then ten, without any signs of it ringing.

Maybe the principal hadn't managed to get back to her immediately.

"Sakuta, you'll catch a cold."

Kaede had been watching a video lecture on her laptop at the *kotatsu*. She had a point; it was hardly the season to stand around in your underwear.

Sakuta headed back to his room to get dressed.

Naturally, *that's* when the phone finally rang.

"Kaede, get that!"

"Ugh, again?"

But he heard her getting up and her feet stomping across the room. Three and a half steps to the phone. At which point, it stopped ringing.

"They hung up!"

He finished changing and went back to the living room.

Kaede slipped back into the *kotatsu*, and he took her place by the receiver.

He reached for the button to check the last number, and it rang again. An eleven-digit number starting with 070.

Sakuta picked up the phone.

"Azusagawa speaking."

"Oh. Uh, I'm Himeji, Azusagawa-sensei's student."

She sounded a little tense.

"Himeji? It's me."

"Whew! Glad it's you, Teach!"

"You sure are making a big deal over a simple call. Why'd you hang up the first time?"

"Who actually dials a landline these days? I got all nervous and accidentally hung up."

"Fair enough."

He didn't own a cell phone, so he didn't really get that.

"Teach, you have got to get a phone," she grumbled. "It was a nightmare getting your number from the cram school."

"Sorry about that. I should have mentioned it earlier. Oh, but you could have just gone through Koga?"

"I *can't* do that twice," she said, sounding very firm on the matter.

This must be a matter of principle for her, but it made no sense to him. He didn't see how it would hurt to ask. She'd simply forgotten to ask his number the last time they'd met.

"Point is, this was awful!"

Even over the phone, he could tell she was sulking.

"Them's the breaks. You said this was about our next lesson?"

"That was just an excuse to get your number."

"Then what's this actually about?"

No use beating around the bush. He heard Sara take a deep breath.

"I wanted to apologize for my poor behavior yesterday."

Her whole tone changed, and she sounded suitably chagrined.

"No need. You weren't out of line at all. I was actually pretty pleased."

"Huh?"

"You were all, 'I've *got* a teacher.'"

"Augh! Forget I said that!"

Her voice went up and then died back down. He barely made out the end of it.

"But you could have said all this at our next class."

Certainly wasn't worth going through all the trouble of getting his number.

"I couldn't wait. I had to get this done ASAP."

"Seriously, I wasn't upset."

"You should be! It's like I don't matter to you."

"You do matter, which is why I think you should give serious consideration to what we talked about yesterday."

"You mean Futaba's classes?"

He could tell she didn't even wanna talk about that.

"It doesn't have to be her specifically, but I think it would be better for you to have a teacher at your level."

"I've been thinking about that."

This sounded like a suggestion.

"What?"

"What if you got yourself to *my* level, Teach?"

She intentionally made her voice sound pompous.

"I think my level's capped."

"You can do it! I'm cheering for you!"

He certainly didn't mind hearing that. It even made him want to try. But he didn't go so far as to make promises.

Sara's decision in this matter could affect her college plans. It'd be best if he avoided saying anything careless and let her think on it some more. They should talk it through properly.

"Himeji, do you have time tomorrow afternoon?"

"Where'd that come from?"

"I figured we should meet up and talk about this."

"I suppose. Oh, but…tomorrow…"

"Not a good time?"

It sounded like she had plans.

"No, just…"

She sounded weirdly reluctant. Choosing her words—searching for the right phrase.

"If you can't say, fine."

"No, it's okay. I was considering telling you anyway."

"Oh? What's going on?"

"Thing is, Sekimoto-sensei really wants to see me again."

That name threw him for a second, but he dug into his memories and found a match.

"Isn't that your previous…?"

"Yeah. He taught me before you."

What would meeting him mean? At the least, the world would not look favorably on that. She'd switched to Sakuta's class because this Sekimoto had fallen in love with her. There was no telling how he felt now, but either way—those emotions were entirely one-sided. It didn't seem right for Sara to see him at this point.

"Himeji, what time are you meeting him? Where?"

And having heard this news, he couldn't exactly stay uninvolved.

"Five, by Fujisawa Station."

"Got it. Then let's do this…"

He offered up a proposal.

One that made her gasp.

6

The next day was Friday, December 16.

Sakuta had classes through third period. When the bell rang, he left, making a beeline back to Fujisawa Station. He hit the platform just past four thirty, checking the time against the board with the list of arrivals.

He followed the people ahead of him up the stairs and tapped his commuter pass on the gate. He emerged on the overpass outside the north exit and found the sky to the east still technically hanging on to blue. But the sky to the west was turning orange, and evening was rapidly taking hold.

Sakuta sat on a bench in the clearing by the electronics store, watching the encroaching night. Inside ten minutes, the sky had grown noticeably dark, and the lights around the station came on.

For that one moment, the crowds in the square looked up from their phones. With the holiday illumination, the station looked very festive.

The square's clock showed four forty-five.

The man he was here for showed up before it hit 4:46. A man in black slacks and a charcoal coat. Short hair set with gel to keep it tidy. He looked to be around twenty-five.

He glanced around the square, looking for someone. His eyes met Sakuta's, but the man didn't recognize him. They hadn't worked closely together, so that was understandable. Sakuta himself likely would have brushed right past him on the street without realizing who it was.

Not finding the person he was looking for, the man took a seat on the bench across from Sakuta. He took his phone out of his coat pocket, glanced down at it, and tapped the screen a few times. Likely texting "Here" to the person he was meeting.

But she wasn't coming.

Sakuta was here instead.

He stood up and walked directly over. They'd been only ten yards apart to begin with. Sakuta stopped in front of him, and the man looked up with a frown.

"Sekimoto-sensei, right?" Sakuta asked.

"Er, uh…you're…"

The man finally placed him.

"Azusagawa. I work part-time at the cram school."

"Ah, right."

He answered like that cleared things up, but there was still a question in his look. He didn't know why Sakuta would be here, talking to him.

"I'm afraid Himeji's not coming. I'm here in her stead."

"Huh…?"

His eyes opened wide as he finally understood what was happening.

Picking up on the tension between them, a few people nearby glanced their way. No one was looking directly at them, but they were keeping an eye out and obviously listening in.

"I've got nothing to say to you," Sekimoto said, standing up. There was a hint of panic in his voice, and he clearly wasn't keeping his frustration in check, either. He tried to walk away.

"Wait a sec."

"……"

He stopped, as if on reflex. The impulse to hear Sakuta out seemed like a sign that Sekimoto had been raised well. The world might see him as a bad teacher who'd tried to get with a student, but deep down, he had an earnest soul. That's how Sara had snared him. Her playful teasing had gotten its hooks into his heart.

Sakuta kept talking to the man's back.

"Don't try to contact Himeji again."

Sekimoto turned slowly around.

"Don't try to see her again."

Sekimoto took a few steps back his way.

"Don't…"

Before he could finish…

"Don't what?!" Sekimoto yelled, grabbing his shirtfront.

Every eye was on them, but nobody even slowed down.

Sekimoto took two or three heavy breaths, his chest rising and falling.

Sakuta waited for that to settle down a bit before speaking again.

"Don't reply, even if Himeji contacts you."

He looked Sekimoto right in the eye, saying what needed to be said.

"……"

The man's eyes wavered. They were practically swimming. He understood what Sakuta was saying to him.

"I think that's best for Himeji, so if you care about her…please."

Still in the man's grip, Sakuta bowed his head.

Sekimoto's hand loosened and then drifted away, like it had lost its place.

"Has the school heard…?" he asked, addressing the back of Sakuta's still bowed head.

He looked up and found Sekimoto clearly at a loss. He was trying to hide that but couldn't figure out how, and that made him even more lost. There was no way out of this mess. Only Sakuta knew the way to freedom.

"I expect I'll let the principal know the outcome."

"Meaning…?"

"Nothing happened. I don't think it'll be a problem."

"……I'd appreciate that."

This was likely the closest to a thank-you he could manage here.

"Can I ask one thing?"

"Sure."

"Uh…" Sekimoto opened his mouth, then thought better of it. "No, never mind."

The unspoken question had probably been about Sara. Had she said anything about him? How was she doing? Were her grades holding up? Maybe all of those. But he shook his head and wound up saying nothing.

"Then can *I* ask something?"

"……"

Sekimoto didn't agree to that, but neither did he refuse. He couldn't do either.

"You can't wait until she's graduated high school? If you're still interested then."

Sekimoto managed a listless "We'll see." That sounded like he was throwing in the towel. He was simply going through the motions to put up a front and sound like he didn't care. But those motions had meaning. Sometimes humans felt the need to keep up appearances no matter what. If nothing else, that was important to Sekimoto in this moment.

"I'd better go. Look after Himeji."

"I will."

· "And watch yourself."

Sekimoto forced a smile and offered parting words that could be taken as joking or spiteful before turning toward the station, soon disappearing into the crowd.

The eyes pricking Sakuta's back vanished as soon as Sekimoto left. All but one pair...

He turned, looking for the source of that gaze. She wasn't hard to find.

A slender figure, by the flower beds.

Sara, giving him a worried look.

When his eyes met hers, she flinched, as if she'd been caught red handed.

He slowly made his way over.

"You agreed to wait at the school."

"...You lost a button."

Sara's eyes were on his collar. It must have snapped off in the fray.

"I've got a spare."

It came stitched onto the tag.

"I've always wondered what you used those for, but I guess it's times like this."

He turned up the hem of his shirt and showed her the buttons, but that didn't seem to improve her mood. Sara would normally have offered to sew it on for him with an impish grin, and he waited for her usual response, but she said nothing.

"Welp, that's taken care of, so let's finish up that chat from yesterday."

"......Yeah."

Even that was awfully quiet.

Sakuta and Sara were seated on opposite sides of a table topped with a cream soda, a coffee float, and a dish of pizza toast.

They'd stepped into a retro café a few minutes from the station, down a narrow alley.

The chairs, tables, and menus all had a Showa-era vibe. Sakuta hadn't been alive back then, but somehow, it felt nostalgic. Somewhere along the way, the connection between Showa and nostalgia had been implanted in his mind.

The ice in the cream soda melted, and the ice cream sank a bit.

"Don't need a picture?" Sakuta asked, watching it melt. Sara had picked the shop, saying she'd always wanted to go there, but the clientele was mostly grown-ups, so she and her friends had never dared.

Her wish had come true, but she was just sitting there, not even snapping a photo of her drink.

"Can I drink mine?" he asked, reaching for the coffee float.

"Oh, wait! I do want a pic!"

Sara yanked her phone out and took pictures of everything they'd ordered. Still, she looked nowhere near as into it as she'd been with the donuts last time. It was more like a professional obligation. No joy in it.

Half her mind was still on something else.

"......Um, Teach."

She put the phone away.

"Mm?"

"I still...want you for a teacher."

Her eyes were trained on him. She'd been thinking about it the whole time.

"Uh-huh," he said noncommittally.

Sara's gaze fled to the cream soda. She put the straw to her lips and took a sip.

"Is that a no?" she asked, looking up at him.

Now it was his turn to escape to his drink.

"Do you have your heart set on a particular college?" he asked.

"Not yet."

She swirled her straw around. The ice cream sank into the green liquid.

"That makes sense. You're still a first-year."

Sakuta stuck his straw through the ice cream in the coffee float and mixed it in.

"Teach, why'd you pick your school?"

"I wanted to enjoy campus with my girlfriend."

This was so blatant that Sara started laughing. The first smile he'd seen today. It wasn't exactly sunny, yet. There were still clouds over it.

"You really do care about her."

"It's true love."

He met her eyes as he said that, and she jerked away, turning red.

"I'm not talking to *you*, Himeji."

"I—I know that! You just caught me off guard! And I'm a cram school student! At least pretend you had upstanding motives for picking a school."

She was blurting out a lot at once here.

"I try not to lie to students."

"Fine, let me change the question."

He wasn't sure what was fine.

"Teach, why'd you decide to go to college at all?"

"Well…"

"Don't you dare say to spend more time with your girlfriend."

Sara read his mind.

Now he had to give a real answer. It might just be a cram school, but she was still a student, and he owed her that much.

"Fine. I wasn't sure when I was studying for exams, but now? I'm at college to get a teaching license."

"Huh? Teach, you're gonna *actually* be a teacher?"

Sara's voice squeaked with surprise. Her eyes rarely opened that wide.

"Well, I'm gonna get the certificate at least. Not really sure it's for me. Oh, keep this a secret—I ain't told anyone yet."

"Not even your girlfriend?"

"Nope."

"Or Futaba-sensei?"

"Not her, either."

This was true. He had nothing against telling them, but it hadn't come up. It would be weird to just announce it, so he'd been leaving it to the right moment.

"Then this is a secret just between you and me, Sakuta-sensei."

Sara seemed delighted. She seemed a bit more like herself again.

"But if you're gonna actually teach, you definitely have to level up."

"I think part of being a good teacher is considering your students' futures and giving them appropriate advice."

"Do you hate teaching me that much?"

Sara looked up at him, stirring the ice cream around her glass.

"Of course not."

Sakuta reached for a slice of the pizza toast and took a big bite.

"Then..."

"But I do think you should try out other teachers. For your own sake."

"……"

"If you find a teacher you like better than me, switch to them. If you don't, then I'll just have to get better. Sound like a deal?"

"……You don't care if I pick some other teacher?"

She was still stirring her cream soda. There was no longer a distinction between the cream and the soda. Sara's eyes refused to budge from that glass.

"If your scores get better than they are now, then as your former teacher, I'd be tickled pink."

"Even if *you* didn't teach that stuff?"

"That part doesn't really matter to me."

"So I don't really matter to you."

"What matters to me is how much I can help *you* out. As your part-time cram school instructor."

"Is that really how you think?"

"It is," he said. No hesitation.

"......"

Sara was staring fixedly at him.

Paying that no heed, Sakuta took another bite of pizza toast. He'd meant every word he said, so there was no need to beat around the bush. Or any reason to overexplain himself.

Sara might be studying without any clear purpose now, but eventually, she'd probably find one. And when that happened, he didn't want her regretting the choice she made now. She was already a bright student, so it couldn't hurt to focus on improving some more. That would give her more options in the future. Whether he was personally involved in that improvement was irrelevant. He would always choose what made her future a richer one.

"......Sakuta-sensei, I get that you're taking my life seriously," Sara said after a long silence. She slurped up the rest of her cream soda. When the glass was empty, she added, "So I'll take your advice to heart."

She didn't look entirely convinced by it. She knew he had a point, but it didn't match up with how she felt. And her tone and pursed lips proved she wasn't happy that this conversation hadn't gone her way.

"I think that's for the best," he said, nodding.

Sara avoided his gaze, escaping to the windows.

"But if I can't find a better teacher, I will come back to you."

"In that case, you'll have to help me grow as a teacher."

"Fine! That works for me!"

Sara smiled, but the clouds had not fully cleared. He figured it would take a while before it all sank in.

And as she stared out the window, he felt her profile looked determined. Like her mind was already on the next step. And he was pretty sure that was not a figment of his imagination.

He paid the check, and they stepped out. "Thanks," Sara said, bobbing her head.

They walked together toward the station. To her bus stop.

Neither spoke at first.

Eventually, they got stuck at a walk light, and Sara said, "Oh! Sakuta-sensei."

Her voice was oddly cheery.

"Mm?" he asked, wondering what was up.

"Have you figured out your homework yet?"

"Homework?"

The light turned green, and they hit the crosswalk.

"Don't act like you don't know. My Adolescence Syndrome!"

"Oh, that. No clue whatsoever!"

"Sakuta-sensei, you're not even trying to solve the problem."

She grinned triumphantly, like she saw right through him.

"......?"

She'd definitely hit the nail on the head, which only deepened his suspicions.

"You're trying to work backward and cure my syndrome that way."

"......"

Sara was really driving that point home, and it made his heart skip a beat. The surprise itself passed quickly but left him drowning in an ocean of questions, an icy note of fear taking over. Sara might be a smart girl, but he didn't see how she'd worked that out.

Before they reached the bus stop, Sakuta paused in the drop-off circle beneath the pedestrian overpass.

"For your own sake, I think you're better off *not* curing my Adolescence Syndrome," she said, stopping a few paces ahead.

"What do you mean?"

Both were bathed in the orange light of the setting sun.

Sara's smile didn't reach her eyes as she turned to face him.

"I looked it up. They call this remote viewing."

She had her phone in her hand.

"Remote viewing?"

That wasn't a phrase he was familiar with.

"No matter how far away I am, I know what someone is doing and thinking."

"......"

"So I know a lot of your secrets, Sakuta-sensei."

"The only secrets I have are that teaching-license thing and maybe my PIN number."

"And the fact that you're searching for Touko Kirishima."

"......"

"Surprised?"

"Honestly, I'm flabbergasted."

"I also know your PIN number. It's your girlfriend's birthday!"

"Do you also know what color underwear I have on?"

"That's just inappropriate!" she said, her anger looking fairly genuine. "Don't worry—I'm not peeping on you in the bath."

Sakuta didn't really mind if she did, but he figured saying so would be even more inappropriate.

"That idea is *totally* inappropriate," Sara said, blushing slightly.

So much for freedom of thought.

"Back to the point—Himeji, do you know where Touko Kirishima is? Or what she's doing?"

"Not at all."

That wasn't the answer he'd been expecting. Her attitude had suggested she did, so what was going on here?

"I can't view just anyone. Only people I've met—and bumped pretty hard."

She swung the hand holding her phone, demonstrating.

"Ah, quantum entanglement." '

"What's that?"

Sara blinked at him. This cleared up one thing—she might be able to read his conscious thoughts, but she didn't have access to his memories.

Reading that thought, she nodded.

"Quantum entanglement is a mysterious phenomenon that occurs at the microscopic level. I didn't really follow the explanation beyond that."

The details weren't actually all that important.

He had other things to think about.

Like how to take advantage of Sara's Adolescence Syndrome.

Used right, this could give him some insight into Touko Kirishima's mind.

And he had to admit, that was a real boon.

"Uncured, I can help you out."

"Himeji, could you *see* Touko Kirishima?"

Everything would hinge on that.

"I could! The miniskirt Santa Claus."

The biggest hurdle had already been cleared.

"All you've gotta do is put us together."

"She's not someone you can just meet whenever you want."

Sightings were rare and unpredictable.

"But you've promised to help her with a live broadcast."

He had. Apparently, Sara had been watching that.

"If you call that a promise."

The date was a real problem.

Touko had told him to help her on December 24.

Christmas Eve, the last day he wanted other plans.

"That explains it, right? This is why the two of us were together on Christmas Eve!"

Sara looked pleased with herself, like she'd just solved a difficult problem.

On the other hand, Sakuta just seemed glum.

Was there no way of escaping this twist of fate? He gave it some serious thought but saw no ray of hope. If he could learn something about Touko Kirishima, that was his top priority, even at the cost of a getaway with Mai.

Ever since Ikumi Akagi had relayed that message from the other potential world...until he knew what it meant, he had to pursue any lead.

"Himeji, are you free on the twenty-fourth?"

"If you absolutely insist, Sakuta-sensei, I could make it a date."

"It'll be cold, so dress warm."

That was the sole battle he had a shot at winning here.

7

"This is getting weird."

Relaxing in the tub, Sakuta was talking to himself again.

He glanced at the water and saw his own goofy mug looking back at him.

It really had taken an odd turn.

Yet despite that, two things were clear.

First, the dream he'd had about Christmas Eve. At least now he knew why he'd been with Sara.

Second, the nature of Sara's Adolescence Syndrome.

He hadn't observed any supernatural stuff going on around her, and this explained why.

"Remote viewing..."

She'd said no matter how far away she was, she could tell what someone was doing and thinking. The whole thing took place entirely inside her mind. That *would* make it hard for him to tell.

But what was that like?

If he took what she'd said at face value, she could even see him now, in the bath. But assuming she had kept her word, she was showing discretion and not peeping at him at times like that. In other words, she wasn't viewing him right this instant. Logically, no matter what he did or thought, Sara wouldn't know.

"If the cause really *is* quantum entanglement…"

An idea was forming in his head.

Rio had given him a lecture on quantum entanglement a while back. Two particles that struck each other with a certain degree of force inexplicably began to behave alike. Once connected like that, no matter how far apart, they would always act the same—a baffling fact.

Naturally, all that occurred on a scale too small for the human eye to see.

Rio had insisted it was ridiculous to apply this to a macro level.

But if you chose to be ridiculous, then no matter how far apart he and Sara were, his state would be communicated to her. That's how she could see what he saw and know what he was thinking.

And if that was true, the reverse might be, too.

Could Sakuta share Sara's state?

Maybe he already was.

And just hadn't noticed.

Didn't know they were entangled.

Or didn't believe it.

The truth became manifest when it was perceived.

"Feels like a long shot…"

But he tried closing his eyes.

Naturally, he couldn't see a thing.

All he could hear was the whir of the bathroom fan.

He couldn't see or hear anything else.

This was normal. The natural result. It made sense that things weren't going to be that easy. Sakuta's ideas rarely worked out. Maybe if Rio had suggested it…

But no sooner had that thought crossed his mind than he heard music playing.

"……"

He wasn't hearing things. That *was* music. It felt like he had headphones on. And now he was pretty sure that's exactly what he was hearing.

He'd heard this song before.

It was one of Touko Kirishima's numbers.

He opened his eyes and found his mind no longer in the tub.

He was lying on a bed in an all-new room. Face down, with a pillow as a cushion, playing with a phone.

Looking at winter date outfits.

Obviously excited.

That thrill of anticipation.

There were clear thoughts, too.

——*That's cute.*

——*Would Sakuta-sensei like this sort of thing?*

——*Urgh, I just don't know. What do I go with?*

——*Let's find something better.*

Fingers ran across the screen.

——*Gotta decide where to go.*

——*If we end up at his college…*

——*We hafta hit Kamakura first, yeah.*

——*In which case…*

As if interrupting the stream of thoughts, a voice came from outside the room.

"Sara, take your bath. Or Dad'll go in first!"

"Augh, wait! I'm coming!"

The music stopped, and the headphones popped out.

While getting up from the bed, he caught a glimpse of a cutesy girl's bedroom. The curtain pattern, the little decorations on the desk, complete with a miniature cactus...

The girl opened the closet and grabbed some pajamas and clean underwear. He could see Sara reflected in the mirror nearby.

The entire sequence felt like looking into a mirror and seeing someone else.

He flinched and opened his eyes.

"......"

Back in the old bathroom.

His dumb face still floating on the water.

"I guess *that's* what it feels like."

When Sara had talked about remote viewing, she hadn't meant she could see *him*. She saw what he saw. His thoughts echoed inside her own head.

A strange experience, indeed.

He thought about experimenting further...

But Sara had been about to take a bath, so this was hardly the time. And he'd be better off not letting her know he could view her right back. She probably wouldn't appreciate that.

Sakuta considered what he'd seen.

She was really looking forward to it.

To December 24.

That was what he'd wanted...

But seeing it for himself brought a twinge of guilt. Not a pleasant feeling. He wasn't comfortable with much of this, especially trying to take advantage of her Adolescence Syndrome.

"Yeesh..."

But he couldn't afford to back down.

He didn't intend to either.

"Sakuta, phone call from Mai."

Kaede's voice, outside the door.

"Tell her I'll call her right back!" he said, heaving himself out of the tub. He'd been in the water longer than usual and felt a little light-headed. But he didn't have time to sit around fanning himself. Even in this condition, he had to think fast.

How was he going to tell Mai about the twenty-fourth?

"It'd be great if we could postpone the trip…"

Outside the bathroom, he said a silent prayer and dialed Mai's number.

Chapter
4
december 24

1

December 24.

As Christmas Eve dawned, Sakuta was woken by Nasuno stepping on his face—just past eight, a little later than usual.

If he'd had classes, he definitely wouldn't have made it in time, but the last class on his schedule had been two days prior. He was free until the New Year.

He could stay burrowed in his warm covers, sleeping in as much as he liked. It would have been fine to give in to the temptation. He didn't have any work plans, either. But he did have good reason to force himself out of his comfy bed.

"...Just like the dream."

He checked the clock, saw 8:11 on it, and left his room.

Like the dream, he poured dry cat food for Nasuno.

Then he put a slice of bread in the toaster and fried some sausages in the same pan as the eggs. When those were done, he and Nasuno ate together.

He did the dishes, started the laundry, and headed back to the living room. As he did, Kaede stumbled blearily out of her room.

"Morning, Sakuta."

"Breakfast?"

"Yes, please."

Yawning, she sat down at the dining room table. He put a plate of precooked eggs and sausage, toast, and a panda mug full of cocoa before her.

"Mm? Did I ask for cocoa?"

"Totally."

In the dream.

"Yeah?"

She seemed unsure, but she started tearing pieces off the toast and dunking them in the cocoa. Soon, the only thing on her mind was how good it was.

"Kaede, you're eating lunch with Kano?"

"Did we talk about that?"

"We did."

Also in the dream. All she'd said in real life was that they were going to see Sweet Bullet's Christmas concert. Her friend Kotomi Kano would be with her. In the evening, she wasn't coming back to Fujisawa but was heading to their parents' place in Yokohama for Christmas. She hadn't explicitly mentioned her lunch plans outside of the dream.

"So you'll be leaving just past ten?"

"Yeah. You?"

"Just past noon."

As they spoke, the laundry beeped.

"When you get home, tell Mom and Dad I'll pop by for New Year's," he said, heading down the hall.

"Got it," Kaede said through a mouthful of toast.

He hung up the laundry, vacuumed, saw Kaede out the door, and then started getting ready himself.

Like he'd said, he left around noon.

"Nasuno, mind the fort."

Nasuno stopped washing her face and meowed back.

Sakuta headed to Fujisawa Station, a ten-minute walk from home.

The heart of Kanagawa Prefecture's Fujisawa City, the JR, Odakyu, and Enoden Lines all ran through here.

He knew this station like the back of his hand, but today—well, he'd seen it like this before, in his dream.

The Christmas Eve crowd was just like he'd dreamed it.

Men carrying little gift bags.

Women all dressed up.

People meeting in the square outside the electronics store.

Everyone looking nervous and eager.

Sakuta stood in the thick of the crowd, waiting for Sara.

The crowd gradually thinned as, one after another, their partners arrived.

He checked the clock. It read 12:29.

If the dream was accurate, she should be here soon.

A moment later, a voice came from behind him.

"I'm here."

It wasn't the voice he'd expected.

But it was one he'd know anywhere.

Confused, he turned around.

Definitely Mai, but why?

She had a cap on and her hair in two pigtails dangling in front of her shoulders. Plus the fake glasses she wore when incognito. Beneath the down jacket, he saw a sweater and slacks that resembled denim. On her feet were sneakers, good for walking. She was definitely dressed down.

"Why are you here, Mai?"

The question had to be asked.

"I'm coming with you."

She acted like that was obvious, when it was anything but.

"Huh?"

"I said I'm coming with you."

"I heard, which is why I said, 'Huh?'"

"I'm coming with you."

She was not brooking arguments here. They were stuck in a loop, with no escape. Mai had her mind made up and was making that very clear. She was not seeking Sakuta's consent, nor was she remotely interested in his opinions on the matter. It was simply a proclamation. There was nothing left to discuss. The matter was set in stone.

"Mai, when we talked about this on the phone, you said, 'Okay.'"

"And I got ready to go."

Mai jammed her hands into the pockets of her down jacket and struck a fashion model pose. Demanding feedback.

"Mm, you're super cute again today."

"You don't even mean that."

She reached out and pinched his cheek.

He did mean it. He thought she looked cute. But he was so rattled that it was hard for him to show any other emotions.

How was he supposed to explain this twist to Sara?

He had no clue.

"Um…Sakuta-sensei?"

She arrived before he could think of anything.

His eyes turned ninety degrees and found the girl he'd actually been waiting for. She'd stopped a good three yards out. Like he'd suggested, she was dressed warmly. She was looking from Sakuta to Mai to her fingers on his cheek. Her expression suggested that she was well beyond simple surprise.

"I'm parked over there," Mai said, letting go of his cheek and walking off toward the south exit.

"What's going on?" Sara hissed.

"Sorry. I just found out myself," he managed. This hardly explained anything, but all other words failed him. He wasn't hiding things and had told no lies. If Sara was viewing him now, she knew he really was at a loss.

"Come on, Sakuta."

Mai was already ten yards off, in a rush.

"Mind coming with?" he asked.

"O-okay…"

Sara was clearly just caught up in the flow.

2

Mai's hands on the wheel.

"……"

Sakuta in the passenger seat.

"……"

Sara in the back seat, bolt upright.

"……"

The car left Fujisawa Station and headed south toward Enoshima on Route 467. This would eventually take them to the coast road.

That sounded like a lovely drive, but nobody was saying a word.

There was only the pleasant hum of the car in motion.

Mai was the first to break the silence.

"Sakuta," she said.

"Mm?"

He glanced sideways and found her eyes on the car ahead.

"She seems rather bewildered. Perhaps you'd better introduce us."

He checked the back seat in the rearview mirror. Sara was sitting like a cat stuck in a tree. She hadn't once let her back touch the seat since she stepped into the car.

"Um, Mai."

"What?"

"I'm pretty bewildered myself."

"Why would you be? It's not like I caught you cheating."

"It sure feels like you did."

"That's because you haven't introduced us."

That did seem the only way to relieve this awkward tension.

"Himeji," he said, turning around to look at her.

"Y-yes?" she stammered. She was definitely stressed out by the whole situation.

"I'm sure you're aware, but this is my girlfriend, Mai Sakurajima."

"Of course I'm aware. I've seen her TV shows. The concert scene in her new movie gave me goose bumps."

Even her tone was stiff. Like she was reading a book report in front of class.

"Thank you," Mai said, smiling warmly.

"And this is Sara Himeji, one of my students at the cram school."

Completing the formality.

"She goes to Minegahara, so she's our kohai."

The car stopped at a red light.

Mai turned around and looked Sara right in the eye.

"Nice to meet you," she said.

"Th-the pleasure is all mine!"

Sara was blinking, still astonished this was real. Mai Sakurajima, in the flesh. Right in front of her, moving, talking. And the shock of that was all too obvious.

"Can I call you Sara?"

"Y-yes. Please."

"Feel free to use my first name as well. *Sakurajima* is so long."

"Okay."

"Careful, Himeji. I tried giving her a nickname once, and she nearly killed me."

"I did not."

"You were pretty mad, though."

"Not at all. I was simply disciplining an ill-mannered kohai."

"See? She's furious."

He turned around to address her directly, but Sara wasn't answering. Her mouth was half-open, just barely managing a smile. It was an awkward one. She couldn't exactly agree with Sakuta while Mai could hear her. Or perhaps their no-holds-barred banter was just shocking. That actually seemed pretty likely. He got why.

Before she recovered, Mai asked, "Is Sakuta a good teacher?"

"My students like me more than you'd think."

"I wasn't asking *you*."

"Aww."

Ignoring his disappointment, Mai glanced at the mirror, saying, "Well?"

"Um, his students like him more than you'd think."

"Really?" Mai asked, like she couldn't believe her ears.

If he tried to butt in here, she'd probably just tell him to hold his tongue. Not wanting his student to see that, Sakuta voluntarily chose silence.

"Really. Not just me. His other students—Yamada and Yoshiwa— they've both gone to him for help, too."

"With classwork?" Mai asked.

"Mostly romantic advice. Yamada asked how to get himself a girlfriend."

Sara started laughing halfway through, her stress finally ebbing away.

"What subject do you teach again, Sakuta?"

"I'd *prefer* to teach math."

But for some reason, all the questions he got were about dating.

"I'd argue you're the reason I get these questions, Mai."

If they knew who his girlfriend was, anyone would start to wonder. Math would become a secondary concern. It was only natural.

"Don't blame me."

They got caught at another red light. Once they'd stopped, Mai reached out to pinch Sakuta's cheek again.

"Ow, ow! Ack, look! Mai, the light's changed!"

He pointed ahead at the green light.

Mai let go and eased on the gas, following the car ahead.

"Are you always like this?"

"Like this?" Mai asked.

"Like what?" Sakuta asked, a beat later.

"In perfect sync," Sara said, for lack of a better phrase.

"We're normally even more intimate."

"Don't make it weird when your student is watching."

Despite her words, Mai was smiling. And she didn't seem inclined to refute what he'd said.

Sara clammed up, even more sheepish than before. There was no room for her between them, and that left her in an awkward position.

But while she stalled, the car sped away. The Shonan Monorail station passed on their left. Specifically, the Shonan Enoshima Station. On the right was the crossing for the Enoden Enoshima Station. A train bound for Fujisawa was just running through it.

In a moving car, these things sped by.

On they drove, until they reached an intersection. This one involved not just the roads and sidewalks, but the Enoden tracks. People, cars, and trains went through here. There were houses and shops on either side. This was the stretch right before Koshigoe Station, the sole section of the Enoden Line that ran along the street. A remnant of when it had been a streetcar. Other traffic had to yield to the trains. This stretch of tracks had only remained possible with the cooperation of the locals, and the result was positively picturesque.

But even that atmospheric locale was soon lost in their taillights.

At Koshigoe Station, the road left the tracks behind.

The train followed the tracks, and the cars the road.

The road ran straight off ahead, flanked on both sides by signs advertising whitebait. And just as those petered out—they reached the ocean.

Route 134, a road that followed the coast.

The steering wheel turned toward Kamakura and Zushi.

Glancing right at the driver's seat, he saw the blue of the ocean, glittering in the sunlight, and Enoshima itself off to the rear.

As that distracted him, a green-and-cream train popped up outside the passenger window. The tracks had cleared the stretch that ran between houses, and the train was speeding up, running alongside their car.

The Enoden on his left, the ocean on the right. Only a car could be framed between the two.

He'd seen all these things before, but this was an entirely new perspective.

They matched the train's pace all the way to Kamakura High School Station.

Not long after, they hit another red light.

This was the intersection near Minegahara High.

Sakuta and Mai both glanced up the hill at their alma mater.

"Seen from a car, it feels weirdly new instead of an old haunt."

"Agreed."

They'd been sick of the sight of it, but it felt oddly unfamiliar.

"Oh, this tea's for you, Sara," Mai said, like she'd just remembered.

She pointed at the bottles in the drink holder. There were two of them. Sakuta picked one up.

It was still warm.

"Here," he said, passing it back.

"Thank you," Sara said as she reached out to take it.

"None for you, Mai?" he asked.

There was only one bottle left.

"I'll just have a sip of yours," she said.

He twisted off the cap of the remaining bottle and handed it to her. Keeping one eye on the light, she took a sip. "Thanks," she said and handed it back to him.

He put the cap on and dropped it back in the drink holder.

The whole time, he could feel Sara's eyes on him. It had been like this since they got in the car. She was searching for a chance to speak, waiting, but couldn't quite find one. Her usual outgoing chattiness had subsided completely.

The light turned green, and the car drove on along the coast.

He glanced at the school again and saw several students headed in.

"Are the teams still practicing over Christmas?"

"Oh, that reminds me. Sakuta-sensei, did you see Yoshiwa this week?"

Sara was leaning forward, pouncing on the topic.

"I saw her yesterday, for the makeup class. She said they got to the beach volleyball semifinals but were eliminated there."

But they'd won the third-place playoff. Third place nationwide was nothing to sneeze at.

"She came back crazy tan!"

"She said the weather was so warm most teams ended up playing in their swimsuits."

Juri has explained this without his asking, like it needed to be excused. She'd had a hint of desperation to her voice, her face red for reasons other than the sun.

"What's this about?" Mai asked, sensing some hidden meaning here.

"Yoshiwa's got a crush on a boy, but that boy's got a crush on me. So Sakuta-sensei gave her some advice on how to get his attention."

Sara was clearly amused by the whole situation. Delighted at the opportunity to share one of Sakuta's secrets with Mai. Excited to see where this would lead.

But before she said anything else...

"If I know Sakuta, he just told her to flash her tan lines."

Mai sounded like she was just stating the obvious.

"Wow! Got it in one..."

Sara sounded shocked. Clearly, she hadn't expected her to get that right. It was hardly an answer you'd arrive at with conventional thinking.

"You know me well, Mai."

"It's exactly the kind of thing you'd say. But be careful who you say it to."

"……You really *are* a couple."

Sara leaned back in her seat, the fight going out of her. A sigh escaped her lips.

"What, did you think he was making it up?" Mai grinned, eyes on the road.

"No, just…you're so comfortable with each other. Sakuta-sensei doesn't act like this at school."

"Oh?"

"He's totally doting on you."

Sakuta glanced in the mirror and saw her sulking. She was more childish looking than usual—or perhaps just acting her age.

When Sara caught him studying her, she pointedly turned away.

"Sakuta adores me," Mai said cheerily. It wasn't clear that she'd picked up on Sara's mood, but Sakuta was sure she had. That was a knowing smile. She was intentionally picking words that would needle the girl.

Sakuta was unsure how he should play this.

If there was a preferred answer, he'd love to follow it.

How were you supposed to handle a date with a student when your girlfriend was riding along…?

The car ran along the beach at Yuigahama for a while and turned left just before the Nameri River.

The guide signs said this was the way to Kamakura.

3

They parked in a lot near Kamakura Station.

"This way," Mai said, heading back the way they'd come.

"Where we going, Mai?"

"You'll see."

He wasn't seeing much of anything right now. He was totally lost. All he knew was that they were moving away from the most Kamakura part of Kamakura. Away from Komachi Street, with all its neat shops for tourists, away from Tsurugaoka Hachimangu, which was basically the symbol of Kamakura.

"We don't go this way often," Sara said, looking around as she walked next to Sakuta.

"Here we are," Mai said, a good three minutes later.

She'd stopped outside a simple but fancy-looking shop. It was obviously far newer than the historical surroundings.

"Mai, you mean...?"

He looked at the letters on the sign and saw MONT BLANC.

"I figured it would be a nice gift for Touko Kirishima. Even if it is so Sara can read her mind, you're going to have to smack her once, right?"

"Ah! Distract her with a Mont Blanc, then pow!"

"How strong a hit *is* it?" Mai asked, peering around Sakuta. Sara was hiding behind him.

"Um...," she said, and she mimed it. A decently hard swing. "That should do it."

Like a hearty clap.

"Does it matter where?"

"Anywhere's fine."

"That shouldn't be too tricky, then."

"Getting the Mont Blanc may be a tougher challenge."

There was already a long line outside. And it *was* December 24. Christmas Eve. Couples were everywhere. Even in Kamakura.

There were maybe fifteen pairs ahead of them. Even if each only took a minute, that was a fifteen-minute wait. And based on what Sakuta saw as he glanced through the window, it seemed like one minute was an optimistic estimate. Once an order was taken, they squeezed out the Mont Blanc like soft serve and then settled up the tab. This could take half an hour.

"Then you'd better get in line, Sakuta."

"While you do what?"

"My being here will do no one any good. Nodoka asked me to get those dove cookies and some Kurumicco. I'll borrow Sara for that."

"Huh?"

"Huh?!"

Their surprise overlapped.

"Come on."

Before they could recover, Mai was walking away.

"Uh, I'll see you later?" Sara asked. With no chance to voice an opinion, she wound up trotting after Mai.

"Hope that's okay...," Sakuta said, getting in line. He was reasonably concerned about this turn of events.

His worries lay with Sara.

He didn't think Mai would do anything too crazy, but this situation was arguably already pretty crazy. This was definitely not an everyday occurrence. Sara was in the middle of the sort of thing that only came around once in a lifetime.

Even Sakuta had never dreamed Mai would show up. She had literally not been in the dream.

This sudden burst of the extraordinary was a huge departure from the dreaming hashtag. The prophetic dream was no longer remotely useful.

If anything would help here, it was remote viewing.

He figured Sara wouldn't notice right now.

Being alone with Mai, she wouldn't have the leeway to think about Sakuta. Certainly not enough to stop and spy on him.

Eyes on the Mont Blanc menu, he sent his mind away. Following the thread of entanglement through the darkness. Finding her, reaching out to her mind—and locking in.

This would let him see what he could not.

Mai's back ahead of him, when it was not.

Sara's view of her.

*   *   *

Mai was walking along the road to a shrine.

Sara was following after, matching her pace.

This was Wakamiya Oji, the road leading straight through the heart of Kamakura to Tsurugaoka Hachimangu.

A few dozen yards ahead, he spotted two red torii gates beneath the winter sky.

But Sara wasn't looking at that.

Her entire focus was on Mai, and Mai alone.

——*What am I even doing?*

He could hear Sara thinking.

——*I was supposed to be in Kamakura with Sakuta-sensei.*

——*I wanted to rent a kimono in Komachi.*

——*Force him to say I looked cute.*

——*Take pictures.*

——*Together.*

——*Eat dango.*

——*Look at the pink shell jewelry.*

——*Make him choose.*

——*Buy me a present.*

——*Tea at the temple with the bamboo.*

——*I thought of all these plans, and now they're ruined.*

——*And he's not even looking at me.*

——*Because she's here.*

A rush of anger.

Resentment.

Her eyes were stabbing Mai in the back.

Mai didn't notice. Or—she'd noticed and was pretending not to. Her acting skills *had* made her a household name.

Seen through Sara's eyes, Sakuta couldn't be sure. He just assumed she knew. She'd known before she even showed up this morning.

——*She's got everything.*

——*Tall.*

——*Glossy hair.*

——*Anime face.*

——*Unblemished skin.*

——*Long legs.*

——*Slim waist.*

——*Pretty…*

——*…and she's cool.*

——*Why would* she *be with Sakuta-sensei?*

This train of thought seemed all about Mai, then somehow he got dragged into it. But the abrupt question had no effect on him. He got that all the time. Getting those looks on campus was still a daily occurrence for him.

"Sara, any Kamakura gifts you'd recommend?"

"Mm? Oh, I love Kurumicco. The box and wrapping are cute, too!"

"I bring those by the set pretty often."

——*That's not it, that's not it.*

"……Um, can I ask you one thing?"

"You can ask more than one!"

"Why Sakuta-sensei?"

——*I'm allowed to ask that much, right?*

Sara stopped moving.

Picking up on that, Mai stopped, too, and turned to face her.

"Why what?"

——*Well…*

"You're not exactly in the same league."

"I'm not good enough for him?"

"The other way, obviously! You could be with some suave actor or popular idol!"

——*I* know *they all want to date you, Mai.*

"Would you want to be with someone like that, Sara?"

——*You don't…?*

"Doesn't everyone?"

"Say you're with them. What then?"

——*Huh?*

"……"

——*What's that mean?*

"Brag about it to your friends?"

Mai had the answer already.

——*Yeah. I would. Totally, I mean…*

"……Is that bad?"

"It's fine. Who doesn't wanna brag about their man?"

"……"

Once again, Sara didn't know how to respond.

——*It's fine?*

——*Then why does her saying that feel…*

Without realizing it, her hands were on her heart.

——*…so horrible?*

"Maybe you're the one against that idea, Sara."

Extremely perceptive. As far as Sakuta was concerned, Mai had nailed it. Sara couldn't quite put it in words, but the idea of dating like that felt wrong to her, and that's why she'd asked the question. Voicing the doubt in her heart.

——*That's not… I don't think…!*

Internally, Sara was trying to argue the point, as if vehement denials would get her back in the fight. She was desperately trying to protect *something*. And that something was likely the version of herself she'd spent her life building up. She couldn't let herself admit her own core values were wrong.

That's why Mai's words were lost on her. She couldn't let them get to her, couldn't let them sway her. She still hadn't gotten the answers she wanted and wasn't backing off yet.

"…That's not true," she said, finally getting her words lined up. It was easy to tell that she was lashing out a bit, but that just played right into Mai's hand. Mai had Sara dancing. She was teasing this emotional response from her.

Sakuta wished she'd go easy on the girl. Sara was just a kid. A first-year in high school. But his prayer didn't reach Mai. This far away, he had no means of getting to her.

"Why'd you pick Sakuta as your teacher?"

"Because…"

Sara tried to answer but didn't get far.

"Because he's dating Mai Sakurajima, and that seemed like a nice challenge?"

"……"

Sara's whole mind went white as a sheet. The shock was so strong that every thought left her.

"Well? Think you've got a shot?"

Unable to say a word, Sara simply stared at Mai, unable to tear her eyes away.

———*She really is beautiful.*

That was somehow the first thing that crossed her mind.

———*If he's dating her, why would he look at anyone else?*

She had her answer.

"You know I don't. That's why you're asking."

———*So why…?*

"Yeah," Mai admitted.

———*Why am I…?*

"But everyone else I've put my sights on fell for me. Even if they had a girlfriend!"

———*What am I even saying?*

"But those boys weren't dating *me*."

Mai's attitude never wavered. She was a rock.

"……"

"And those boys weren't Sakuta."

Each line made her seem *more* unshakable.

"……But you never know!"

——*Enough. Stop it! Just stop talking…*

"Fair enough. Sakuta is free to make his choice."

——*I get it already! Stop, before I stop being me!*

Sara's thoughts were shrieks now, echoing painfully. If Mai pressed home with even one more word, she'd shatter—but that didn't happen.

"Sorry, that's beside the point."

Mai chose that moment to back off.

"You asked why I picked Sakuta, right?"

"Yeah…"

Sara managed to croak out an answer that was barely audible.

"Sakuta puts up with all my nonsense while grumbling appropriately. In this line of work, I'm forever changing plans last minute, and we can't exactly be seen in public together. The fact that he acts that way is such a relief. I don't have to stress over it."

Mai was just *sharing*.

"That's why?" Sara sounded lost.

She would be. Mai probably had more to say—a lot more. This barely scratched the surface.

"Also, he always tells me how good my cooking is. And cooking with him is a real joy. And I love it when we eat together, just the two of us."

"……"

Sara's mind was filling with question marks. No clue what she was even hearing.

"He's great about actually saying 'I love you.' Sometimes he could stand to tone it down a little, though."

Mai laughed, obviously recalling a specific moment.

——*I don't get it. At all.*

Mai caught the baffled look in Sara's eyes.

"I have loads more reasons. I could talk about them all day. How he always says 'Thank you' and 'Sorry,' how he has friends who come to help him, how much he cares about them. How great he is at looking after his sister or playing with his cat. And how he worries about his students."

"Does that mean me?"

"You've peeked inside his mind, right? He hasn't thought about anyone but you all day. And he's been totally sidelining me."

"……"

——*That's right! He's been worried. Sakuta-sensei worries about me…*

"He's one of those people who can devote himself to helping others. The whole time, he'll insist he's doing it for his own benefit. The way he twists things around like that…well, it frustrates me sometimes. But I can't bring myself to hate it."

Mai's smile was positively glowing. A real warmth in her gaze.

——*But I don't want him to worry. I want…*

"Does that explanation help?"

"……"

Sara didn't say yes. She was still confused. She still felt lost.

"It's hard to put emotions like these in so many words. But why am I dating him? That answer's easy."

Sara looked up. Eyes on Mai, hoping this would be the answer she needed.

"…Why is that?" she asked.

Mai's whole demeanor softened. Her eyes were so tender.

There was no hesitation, no beating around the bush. Like she'd said, this one was easy. She'd known the answer all along, and it was probably the same one Sakuta would give.

"I'm dating Sakuta so we can be happy together." Mai spoke the words slowly, savoring them. When she finished, she smiled. Then: "He's the only one who makes me feel that way. Maybe that's why I chose Sakuta."

She said this almost as if the idea had only just occurred to her. As if it were a nebulous feeling that had just now crystallized.

"......"

Sara was speechless. Those words and emotions weren't like anything she'd imagined. Mai's words carried a warmth beyond Sara's experience.

——*What...is this?*

That warmth enveloped her.

——*I've never felt...*

Swallowed her.

——*...anything like...*

She was drowning in it.

——*Anything like this.*

Mai gave her a gentle smile. One that showed how happy she was.

"......"

Sara was stunned. Her emotions were shapeless.

——*I can't.*

Quietly, deep within...something shifted.

——*There's no way.*

"If you don't buy it, see for yourself."

"......Huh?"

"Look inside me."

Mai held out her hand, like she wanted to shake.

"Do that, and you'll experience it all firsthand."

——*What now?*

Sara's fingers shook. No doubt, she was unsure of herself.

——*What do I do?*

Looking for answers.

But no one offered any.

She had to find her own answer.

If anyone else provided her one, that was only *their* answer.

Mai reached for Sara's hand.

——*Don't...*

Their hands were three inches apart.

——*Don't!*

Two inches.

——*I said don't!*

One.

——*No…!*

Almost touching.

"No…!" Sara yelped, snatching her hand away. She clutched it with her other hand, like she was guarding something precious.

——*I don't wanna know!*

Sara's violent rejection echoed through Sakuta's head. The thorns of her outburst pricked his heart.

——*I can't win! There's no way I can beat her!*

Like a phone abruptly hanging up, the view vanished, and the sounds went with it.

He tried again, but it was no use.

He couldn't connect to Sara. He didn't know where she was or what she was doing. He could no longer trace her thoughts.

"Okay, next…sorry for the wait."

A clerk with a Mont Blanc menu was looking at Sakuta. And their smile helped drag his mind back to reality.

4

Behind the counter, the freshly piped Mont Blancs Sakuta had ordered were being carefully placed in a takeout box.

He'd settled the tab and was waiting for them to finish when a staff member hesitantly called out, "Um, pardon me, is there an Azusagawa present?"

They were holding a phone in one hand.

"That's me," he said, confused. Nervous. What could this be about?

"Someone called the store looking for you," they said.

This was naturally unprecedented, and they had no idea how to handle this.

"Oh, sorry! I forgot my phone today," Sakuta explained. The truth would just complicate things, so he came up with a convincing lie and took the phone from them. The small receiver looked like an older cell phone.

"Hello?" he asked.

"Sakuta?"

He placed the voice instantly.

"Mai? What's up?"

"Sorry. I lost Sara."

"Huh?"

"I was paying for our souvenirs, and she was gone. I checked the area but couldn't find her."

Mai was talking faster than usual.

"Where are you?"

"The dove cookie shop."

That was on Wakamiya Oji, between here and Tsurugaoka Hachimangu. He could be there in ten.

"Then wait right there—I'll come to you."

"Sorry!"

"We'll find her."

Sakuta hung up. He asked permission, then quickly dialed a number he'd only just learned. Sara's cell.

No answer on the first call.

Or the second.

The third call picked up just before it went to voice mail.

"……"

She didn't speak, but he could hear her and the noises around her.

"Himeji? It's me."

She hung up before he finished. He heard a gasp.

He gave it one more shot.

"......"

But no matter how long he waited, it didn't connect. Soon enough, he got the automated "I'm unable to answer the phone right now" message.

It didn't seem like trying again would change much.

Sakuta thanked the staff member and returned the store phone.

"Sorry," he said. "I'll be back for the Mont Blanc later. Can you hold on to it for now?"

"Uh, sure...we can do that, but if you take too long..."

He knew why they were hesitant. These expired awfully quick. While he was in line, he'd worked out that this store was a sister shop to the one Touko had taken him to—so their Mont Blancs were also only good for two hours.

"I'll be right back," he said, and he left the shop empty-handed.

Kamakura on Christmas Eve was packed everywhere, even on a big road like Wakamiya Oji. The farther he went, the thicker the crowds got.

He kept an eye out for Sara as he headed to Mai's location. But with crowds this thick, it was hard to even walk straight, much less find someone.

And he reached his destination without spotting her.

The dove cookie shop boasted striking white walls and old-fashioned curtains over the doors. The building was designed to fuse Kamakura's style with the modern age. Inscribed in black on the wall was the name of their signature product—it really drew the eye.

Mai spotted him coming and ran over, apologizing again.

"I might have pushed her a bit too hard," she said, looking suitably chagrined.

"You know where any kimono rental shops are?"

"There's several on Komachi," she said, taking out her phone and checking. "Yeah, see?"

She showed him a map with pins in three or four spots.

"I'll go check those. Mai, you check the *dango* shops and anywhere that sells pink shell jewelry."

"Got it."

"Meet back here when you're done."

Mai just nodded, not asking why.

A glance at the map had given him a general idea of where the stores were, and Sakuta checked each in turn. Komachi was packed with stores, and tons of couples and families were in every single one. Sometimes foot traffic slowed to a standstill.

Even when he managed to reach a shop, there was no sign of Sara. Being Christmas Eve, every store had couples lining up to change into kimonos.

He finally found a lead at the third store.

Not many customers arrived solo, so the staff remembered a girl matching Sara's description. She'd finished changing not five minutes earlier and left the shop.

He'd just missed her.

Sakuta thanked them and rushed back out onto Komachi.

He looked both ways but saw no sign of her. With crowds like this, you could barely see five yards in any direction.

You might even lose a grown-up if you took your eyes off them.

Sakuta headed back, checking each shop as he went.

Mai would probably be doing the same.

His assumption turned out to be correct; when he reached the dove cookie shop, he found her coming from the other direction.

She was shaking her head.

"Any luck on your end?" she asked.

"She did rent a kimono."

"So she's still in the area."

"Probably."

What other clues did he have? What other thoughts had he heard?

"Mai, do you know a temple with bamboo?"

"Hokokuji?"

"Where is that?"

"It's a pretty long walk. And we're carrying stuff. We should drive there."

She showed him the gift bag, then started walking toward the car.

"Mai, let me," he said, taking the larger bag from her.

Inside the yellow-and-white paper bag was a larger yellow can with a dove on it.

"Bring that to your family for New Year's."

"You aren't coming?"

"Of course I am. Gotta wish them a happy New Year."

Without further chatter, they hustled back to the car.

The trip to the car took ten minutes, and so did the drive to the temple. The lot near the entrance was jam-packed.

"That looks full—Sakuta, get out and go ahead on foot."

Checking there was no one on their tail, he opened the door and jumped out. Already the air felt different. They were far from the bustle of Wakamiya Oji and Komachi Street.

When he kicked a stay pebble along the asphalt, it sounded far too loud.

He hurried through the gates onto the grounds.

Inside, the hush only grew more palpable.

Feeling the quiet weighing on him, he pressed forward, spying the bamboo grove up ahead. It was bright green even in the winter chill, full of life.

That drew the eye upward.

Sunlight was streaming between the bamboo leaves. It made the whole place glimmer and feel like he was looking up from underwater. It was magical, almost as if he'd slipped out of this world.

On a narrow path flanked—and topped—by bamboo, he found someone else also peering upward. She wore a kimono, and coupled with the surroundings, it made for a striking scene.

He almost didn't recognize her. It took him a moment.

The kimono was white with red flowers. Her hair had been done up to match.

But this was who he'd been looking for.

"Even at Christmas, bamboo's pretty great," he said.

It made for an unorthodox Christmas tree.

Sara turned around, hairpins swaying.

"Sakuta-sensei! Why...?"

"If you want me to find you, you really should've picked an easier location."

If he hadn't cheated, he probably wouldn't have pulled it off. Finding her would've been impossible.

He took a few steps toward her.

"Don't...!"

Three steps out, a wave of panic hit her, and she turned to run.

"Dressed like that..."

Before he could finish, her hem caught on the stone path, and she went down on hands and knees, like a little kid.

"Ow..."

He was with her in a second.

"You okay there?" he asked, helping her up.

"......I got the kimono dirty."

She brushed off the knees, not brightening up at all.

"I'm asking about *you*."

Sara had hit the ground hard, and her hands were definitely red. Fortunately, the scrape wasn't bad enough to draw blood. He helped brush the dirt off.

"Why...?"

This was likely a very different "why" from the first one.

"My student gets lost, I'm gonna try and find her."

Conscious of the difference, he chose to answer the first question.

"I don't mean..."

Why wasn't he mad at her for vanishing?

Why didn't he demand an explanation?

That was what Sara's second "why" meant.

But Sakuta didn't see the point in discussing that. Knowing the answer wouldn't salvage the situation for her. Instead, he said what he had to say.

"We need to come up with a plan."

"For what...?"

Sara definitely wasn't following his line of thought.

"Himeji, you need a good excuse to head-butt Touko Kirishima."

That was the actual goal here. But her face fell.

"I said it didn't have to be the head...," she murmured, avoiding his gaze. She didn't sound too confident.

"Then why'd you hit me there?"

He and Sara had bumped heads once, before she became his student.

"That's when you started reading my mind, right?"

"I didn't mean to hit you that hard! I can't believe you even remembered it."

"You've got a pretty hard head. Definitely memorable."

"That's the last thing I wanna hear..."

Sara's voice shrank away.

"Okay, how's this for a plan? I open the Mont Blanc box and hold it out to Touko Kirishima. While she's looking inside, you give her the bonk."

"......Um, Sensei."

"I leave the head-butt angle up to you."

"......I can't."

"No? Fair enough, let's think of a plan B."

A breeze passed through the thicket, rustling the bamboo leaves.

"No, I mean," she blurted, talking over him, "I can't do it anymore."

"......"

"I can't see anything."

Her voice was a rasp.

"I can't hear a word."

Sara hung her head sorrowfully.

"I don't know what you're thinking. I can't hear Yamada or Yoshiwa or anyone else. That's what spooked me so bad that I ran off. I'm so sorry..."

"Should we try knocking heads again?"

He held out his forehead, but Sara didn't perk up. Eyes firmly on the ground, she gently bumped her head against his chest. Like a cat rubbing against him.

"Why...why can't I hear them anymore...?"

Two, three times she bumped him.

The second was stronger, the third stronger still.

"Why...?!"

Sara herself knew the reason. She'd figured it out as she talked to Mai. How she felt. What it was she really wanted.

Before she could bump him another time, Sakuta put a hand on her forehead, like he was taking her temperature.

"Let go!"

"If you keep hitting your head, you'll lose all your brain cells."

"Still..."

"Congrats."

"Don't celebrate!" Sara's voice rose to a squeak.

"Curing Adolescence Syndrome is a *good* thing," Sakuta said, in a much more normal tone.

"No it isn't! How am I supposed to help you now?!"

"Don't sweat it."

"I *want* to help you, Sakuta-sensei! I wanted it to be thanks to me! Now there's no point in me being here at all!"

"I'm already grateful you chose to become my student."

"I don't want to be *just* a student!!"

Sara wasn't running from her feelings anymore. She was laying it all out there. And that's why it hit Sakuta so hard. It felt like a hand clamped around his heart—because his answer was set in stone.

"Honestly, it's a bit of a relief."

"……"

"I'm glad I don't have to *use* your Adolescence Syndrome."

He meant every word of that.

It had been bugging him ever since they made those plans.

Sara likely knew that.

And Mai had almost certainly worked it out—which was why she'd joined them.

"So I'm glad you're cured."

"Why…?"

"I mean it when I say: thank you."

"You know what I did with my Adolescence Syndrome! I was spying on everyone! Toying with their emotions—and you know why I was coming after you! How can you just be nice to me?!"

"Well, that's the kind of person I want to be."

"You should be mad! Or at least upset! Now I don't know what to do! You're not fair, Sakuta-sensei. None of this is."

"Grown-ups aren't really fair. Not in my experience."

"Now you're acting like I'm a kid! We're only three years apart!"

"I'm three whole years more grown-up than you, Himeji."

"……So not fair."

Sara's head stayed down, and she sniffed once, like she was fighting back tears.

She did that again and again, her shoulders heaving.

But in time, she settled down.

"Sakuta-sensei," Sara said, her voice choked up.

"What, not done grumbling about me?"

"I'll never stop doing that."

At last, her head lifted. Her eyes still wet with tears, she caught his gaze and held it. There was a determined gleam in her eye.

"I wish I'd been able to fall in love with you properly."

"Our teaching manual says not to get romantically involved with students."

"In that case…"

Sara wiped her eyes with her fingers.

Then forced a grin.

"If I get into my first-choice college, I'll ask you again."

She was setting up an appointment two years ahead.

This was the same advice Sakuta had given Toranosuke. He hadn't expected it to come back to haunt him.

"Brilliant idea," he said.

He had only himself to blame.

"So how long are you gonna snuggle?"

He turned at that voice and found Mai holding her keys and looking cross.

"You have everything, Mai! Let me borrow Sakuta-sensei for a minute. I'm younger—you can afford to indulge me a little."

Sara was certainly not holding back here.

It seemed like a huge weight had lifted off her shoulders.

"Sakuta belongs to *me*," Mai said firmly. She headed back the way she'd come.

But a few steps later, she turned back to Sakuta and Sara.

"You've still got to get to the college and find Touko Kirishima, yes?"

"Oh, right. I guess I do."

That was today's entire goal.

He no longer had any way of reading her mind, but he still had things he had to know.

5

They returned Sara's kimono to the shop, picked up the Mont Blancs, and left Kamakura behind.

They'd been driving for fifteen minutes now.

It was almost four.

But the campus was still out of sight.

"It doesn't seem like we'll get there in time."

"Sorry! If I hadn't…"

Sara was shrinking in the back seat.

"Himeji, can you look up Touko Kirishima on your phone?"

Telling her not to worry about it wouldn't help, so he gave her a job to do instead. Better than just sitting there.

"Okay!" she said, beaming as she pulled out her phone.

A moment later, he heard a sharp breath.

"What?"

"It's already started."

As she spoke, the song started streaming from her phone's speakers.

It was a pleasant, Christmassy song, with lots of bells.

Sara held up the phone so Sakuta could see.

It was showing some sort of garden. A little bridge over a pond. In the distance, on the bridge, was a miniskirt Santa, her back to the camera. Only her outline was really visible.

"That's the garden on campus."

He and Mai were students there, so it was easy enough to place. This was right in the center of the C-shaped main building. The view from their classroom windows was right here on-screen.

The GPS showed they still had a bit over a mile to go before they reached school. Less than five minutes.

But the Christmas song playing on Sara's phone seemed unlikely to last that long. Most songs were four or five minutes, at most. Plenty were in the three-minute range.

Through the windshield, he could see the Keikyu Line. Kanazawa-hakkei Station was up ahead.

The streets and views near their college.

"Approaching your destination," the GPS said.

He could see the main gates, so the notification was unnecessary.

Mai stopped right in front.

"Go on ahead."

"Oh, I'm coming!" Sara hopped out after him.

They went through the main gates onto campus.

The Christmas song on Sara's phone was no longer playing.

But Sakuta hurried toward the garden, careful not to destroy the Mont Blancs he was carrying.

Sara tagged along behind.

"Sakuta-sensei, the live stream's over!"

"Then we can walk right up to her."

He didn't want to accidentally get in the shot and have his face streamed worldwide.

He cut through the building itself, down the hall and out the back door.

Sakuta's gaze snapped to the center pond and the bridge over it. The miniskirt Santa was walking toward him.

Touko spotted him soon enough.

"You're late! It's over."

"You should have waited! I brought refreshments and everything."

He handed over the Mont Blanc box.

"……"

"It's not poison, I swear. But it will expire soon."

"Then I'd better eat it now."

Touko opened the box. The Mont Blanc she took out was in a paper cup, like ice cream. She dug in.

"That was good. What a lovely Christmas present. Thanks."

With that, she walked right past him.

"Nene Iwamizawa, right?" he asked, throwing the question at her back. This was one of the things he'd wanted to confirm.

"……"

She didn't answer, but she did react. Touko stopped in her tracks.

"International liberal arts major, third year. Won the grand prize in the beauty pageant last year. Born March thirtieth in Hokkaido. And you're five foot three."

None of this made her turn around. She kept her back to him.

"I'm Touko Kirishima," she said quietly.

But firmly.

This was maybe the single most emotional thing he'd heard from her.

The tension felt like a knife pressed against his throat.

He didn't know why.

But there was undoubtedly something deeper at play.

Something she was hung up on.

"Um, Sakuta-sensei…?" Sara asked on the other side of her.

"What?"

"Who are you talking to…?"

She looked frightened.

Touko walked right past her. Sara should have seen this, but she didn't react at all. She just stared grimly up at Sakuta.

Sara couldn't see her. Couldn't perceive her.

Touko vanished into the school building.

"……Is she still here?" Sara asked, peering around.

"She's gone now."

"But she *was* here?"

"Yeah."

"But I didn't see anyone. I could see her when I was connected to you, but…"

"That's probably why."

"Huh…?"

"You could see what *I* could see."

He only understood because he'd tried remote viewing himself. He'd been sharing Sara's eyesight. And hearing. All her senses.

He saw what she saw, heard what she heard, and felt what she felt. So when he'd seen Touko, Sara had, too. But with her own eyes—she couldn't see a thing.

"Then…either way, I couldn't have helped."

Sara caught on quick, and her shoulders slumped.

"What a disaster," she said with a sad smile.

"Better than getting all fired up and whiffing in the moment," Sakuta pointed out.

She made a face at him, but resignation soon set in.

"I guess," she admitted, nodding. "I really didn't do *anything*."

She spoke from the heart.

"It's Christmas Eve, and *nothing* good happened."

"Well, we'll have to buy you some cake on the way home, then."

"Really? That works!"

Sara clapped her hands, delighted. This was obviously an attempt to please him. That side of her wasn't likely to change anytime soon. But…that's just who Sara was.

Last Chapter

Holy Night

Sakuta was looking up at the half-moon at the heart of a natural landscape painting, framed by the awning above and the blinds on either side.

The moon floated alone in a jet-black sky.

Like the moon, Sakuta was alone in the outdoor bath.

No sounds of human life.

Like he was alone in the world.

All he could hear was the gentle breeze.

That and the windswept leaves.

And the bubbling of the water flowing into the bath.

These gentle sounds were a balm for the soul.

"This is great."

The words slipped out of him.

The view from the deck was picturesque, and the natural hot springs flowed into the bath attached to their room—both were his alone.

How could he not enjoy it?

They'd dropped Sara back at Fujisawa Station and headed to the inn in Hakone. Mai had called ahead to let them know they'd be late.

It was almost eight when they arrived, but the staff welcomed them warmly.

Sakuta and Mai sat down to a luxurious meal and, after a brief break, went to enjoy the hot springs.

"Having an outdoor bath in your own room…what could be better?"

When they'd arrived, the second he saw the exterior, Sakuta felt like nobody would ever stay here alone. That impression only got stronger as he stepped onto the grounds, when he saw how big the garden was, and when they reached the room.

He was astonished that the room came with a private outdoor bath, but the biggest surprise was that the room had a second story. The first floor was a living room, and the bedrooms were upstairs. Each "room" in this place was practically a house.

He quietly inquired as to the price, but Mai merely said it was a suitable match for her birthday present.

Sakuta chose not to press for specifics. Some things were best left unknown. He was here already, so he might as well enjoy it. There was no point holding back now. They had to take full advantage of the money spent.

As these thoughts ran through his mind, the sliding door rattled open.

These glass doors divided the room from the deck.

"Well? How's the water?" Mai asked. She was in the yukata and haori the inn provided. Her hair was freshly washed and done up in a loose bun.

"It's great."

"Good."

"How was the big bath?"

"I had the place to myself, so it was quite relaxing."

"Maybe I'll go have a swim later."

The bath in their room was hardly big enough. It was exactly the right size for two grown-ups to stretch out in. On his own, Sakuta could spread his limbs all he wanted.

"Don't. I'd rather not be banned."

She looked at least 50 percent serious.

Perhaps she thought he was in a mood to actually do that. She had a point; if she hadn't said anything, his base instincts might have taken hold. The thrill of this stay was totally going to his head.

"If you'd get in with me, I'd have nothing to gripe about," he said.

He cast a baleful glare back at the room. Mai's manager, Ryouko, had just come in. Her face was flushed from the heat, and she was fanning herself with one hand.

"Ryouko checking in ahead is the only reason our reservation didn't get canceled."

Mai's look clearly meant "Be grateful."

"I am grateful!"

But said aloud, it sounded more put out than he'd expected.

"I guess it's fine. It's cold, so not for long."

"What, really?"

He looked shocked, and Mai took off her *tabi* socks and stepped barefoot onto the deck. "Chilly!" she said, and she tiptoed over to the edge of the bath. She sat down sideways on a dry section of the bath's rim. As she did, she grabbed the hem of her *yukata* and deftly pulled it up to knee height. A daring move that made his heart skip a beat.

Oblivious to his response, Mai proceeded to put her feet knee-deep in the bath.

Her legs dangled to one side, gleaming.

The way her hair was done seemed oddly sexy.

Seen through the steam rising off the bath, Mai had a very mature allure.

"Enough for you?" she asked, careful not to get her *yukata* wet.

"Um, Mai."

"What? Is that a no?"

"The opposite. Nothing could be better."

He was so excited he gave her two thumbs-up.

"Don't make waves. You'll get me wet."

Mai raised one leg just enough to kick them back his way.

The spray caught him in the face.

"Oof!"

He wiped the water away. Mai was laughing.

"Oh, right. We just got a text from Futaba," she said, pulling her phone out of her haori pocket.

"What'd she say?"

"If you're with me, she wants to steal a minute. Wanna give her a call?"

Mai held out the phone.

"This is probably about you-know-what," he said.

And that meant he didn't really want to call. But when he took the phone, it was already ringing.

He held it to his ear, listening.

She picked up quick.

"Hello, Futaba speaking."

She sounded polite, likely because given the number, it could have been Mai herself.

"Uh, it's just me," Sakuta said.

He heard a huge sigh. Not relief or disappointment. This was a warning she was about to grumble.

"Azusagawa, did you put that idea in Kasai's head?"

"What'd he do?"

If Toranosuke's dream came true, Rio had given him her answer today.

"I told him I couldn't date a student, and he asked me to reconsider once he'd been accepted to his first choice."

"Huh, smart move, Kasai."

"It sounded like one of your lines, so I figured you put him up to it."

"I wouldn't have gone with *reconsider*. I'd have said 'Go out with me then.'"

That was actually the line he'd fed Toranosuke. The boy must have found that too pushy and had softened it up a bit. Perhaps he simply couldn't bring himself to actually say the words.

"Then you'd better step up."

"How so?"

"You think I can keep teaching him after that?"

"It could be awkward, yeah."

If he passed the exam, he'd planned to ask her out again. But it was Rio's job to teach him what he needed to do that, which was a major conflict of interest.

"So you'd better take over and ensure he passes that test."

Ominous.

"But wait, wasn't his first choice…?"

"Same school I'm at."

A national college with a very high rejection rate. Sakuta could never have made it in.

"That's all. Tell Sakurajima I'm sorry for interrupting. Bye."

"Wait, Futaba…"

The line went dead. She'd already hung up. And the call length had been exactly one minute.

He silently handed the phone back to Mai.

"What'd she say?"

"Sorry for interrupting."

"Okay."

Not just that, obviously, and Mai knew it. But she didn't ask the rest. She probably thought she didn't need to.

They were at a hot springs in Hakone.

Sakuta and Mai together.

Not *just* them, but still…a tranquil moment together.

And she wanted to revel in it.

So did Sakuta.

But nothing lasts forever.

"Okay, get out before you catch a cold," Ryouko said, disturbing their peace. She was giving them a look from the sliding door. It was very much the warm gaze of a grown-up chaperoning a giddy young couple.

But that only highlighted how fulfilling this moment was.

"Thanks for today, Mai."

She looked momentarily thrown but didn't ask for what. Instead, she smiled and said, "You're welcome."

They were happy.

This was their happy place.

That night, sleeping forlornly alone in the first-floor living room, Sakuta had a dream. One so real it felt like it was actually happening.

Many a young person shared the same dream.

A ton of students at Sakuta's college.

A bunch from Minegahara High.

Tomoe among them.

And Rio.

And Nodoka.

Kaede had the dream, too.

And Uzuki.

And Ikumi.

And Sara with them.

Kento, Juri, and Toranosuke all had the same dream.

When she woke up the next morning, Mai alone had seen nothing in her sleep.

afterword

See you next time, in *Rascal Does Not Dream of Santa Claus.*

Hajime Kamoshida